EX LIBRIS
SOUTH ORANGE
PUBLIC LIBRARY
WITHDRAWN

Shades of Simon Gray

Other books by Joyce McDonald

Comfort Creek
Shadow People
Swallowing Stones

Shades of Simon Gray

Joyce McDonald

DELACORTE PRESS

Published by
Delacorte Press
an imprint of
Random House Children's Books
a division of Random House, Inc.
1540 Broadway
New York, New York 10036

This book is a work of fiction. Names, characters, places, and incidents either are the product of the author's imagination or are used fictitiously. Any resemblance to actual persons living or dead, business establishments, events, or locales is entirely coincidental.

Visit us on the Web! www.randomhouse.com/teens
Educators and librarians, for a variety of teaching tools, visit us at www.randomhouse.com/teachers

Library of Congress Cataloging-in-Publication Data

McDonald, Joyce.
Shades of Simon Gray / Joyce McDonald.
p. cm.
Summary: Seventeen-year-old Simon lies in a coma, finding his space and time overlapping with that of a man who was lynched over 200 years ago, while a member of the cheating ring he has been helping wonders if their actions have caused the plagues assaulting their New Jersey town.
ISBN 0-385-32659-9 (hc)—ISBN 0-385-90026-0 (GLB)
[1. Cheating—Fiction. 2. Coma—Fiction. 3. Astral projection—Fiction. 4. Space and time—Fiction. 5. New Jersey—Fiction.] I. Title.
PZ7.M14817 Sf 2001
[Fic]—dc21

2001017424

The text of this book is set in 12-point Fairfield.
Book design by Melissa Knight

Manufactured in the United States of America
October 2001
10 9 8 7 6 5 4 3 2 1
BVG

For my brothers,
Bob, Jack, and Rick

April is the cruelest month, breeding
Lilacs out of the dead land, mixing
Memory and desire, stirring
Dull roots with spring rain.
Winter kept us warm, covering
Earth in forgetful snow, feeding
A little life with dried tubers.

—T. S. Eliot
from *The Waste Land*

Prologue
1798

The four men tracked him down before dawn. He *was sitting beneath an oak tree at the farthermost corner of Joseph Alderman's property, a young man barely twenty, his clothes bloody with the evidence. He showed only mild surprise when the townsmen came upon him. Each of them, in his heart, knew whom the lad had been waiting for.*

One of the men bound the murderer's wrists behind his back with leather thongs, then bound his ankles. Another removed the young man's tricornered hat, slid the noose over his head, and lifted his hair to position the knot behind one ear. He tossed the end of the rope over a low branch, a branch not more than seven feet from the ground, and tied the other end around the neck of one of the horses. The men's movements were quick and efficient.

One of them stepped forward, his face only a few inches from the murderer's. "Do you wish time to pray?" he asked.

The young man said nothing. He looked his executioner straight in the eye. Then one by one, he held the gaze of the other men, until each of them had to look away.

In the gray dawn, mist rose up from the ground, hiding the weeds and tall dry grass. It continued to rise until the forms of the men blurred, gray on gray, their bodies nothing more than darkened shadows in the fog.

They could have put the young man on one of their horses. A stinging swat to the horse's rump and the man would have dropped almost as fast as he would have through the trapdoor of a scaffold; a quick, humane snap of the neck and it would be over. But not one among them wished to have a man with blood on his hands sitting in his saddle, as if the source of the crime were something contagious.

It took three of them, one guiding the horse to step back and two others taking hold of the rope, adding their strength to the horse's, to slowly lift the body eight inches from the ground. The fourth man stood a few feet away, eyes closed, head thrown back, hands extended in a prayer for the soul of the young man who would not pray for himself.

The knot slipped as the men tugged. The rope twisted on itself as the body danced spasmodically until, finally, the toes dropped downward, pointing at the ground. A few minutes later the men stepped forward, untied the rope from the horse, wrapped it around the base of the tree, and secured it in place.

From overhead came a loud rustling noise. Startled, the men looked up into a swirling cloud of black wings, beating at the air. When the cloud settled, the men saw hundreds of crows. They clung to the branches like black leaves. They began to caw, a loud mournful sound that swelled in the early-morning mist and echoed throughout the small town of Havenhill.

The men took wary steps toward each other. They huddled close together. "We are done here," said one.

One of them, the man who had been praying for the murderer's soul, said, "It is now in the hands of the Lord."

The others answered with solemn nods and amens. The good people of Havenhill would rest easy in their beds that night, knowing a murderer was no longer among them.

Chapter 1

On the night Simon Gray ran his '92 Honda Civic into the Liberty Tree, the peepers exploded right out of the local streams, shrieking like souls of the dead disturbed from their slumber, louder and more shrill than anyone in Bellehaven could remember. Like the plague of frogs converging on ancient Egypt, they were everywhere: in window boxes, on front porch rockers, in mailboxes carelessly left open, in gutters. They even clogged a few exhaust pipes.

Most people in town were absolutely positive the peepers caused Simon's accident. With squashed frogs all over the road, their blood, like so much oil, made driving slippery. It was bound to happen to somebody. A few suspected that the sudden appearance of the peepers might be a curse. But this was an unpopular view, Bellehaven being a respectable and upright town.

When the police found no skid marks, nothing to indicate that Simon Gray had slammed on the brakes for dear life, that was no surprise. Everyone knew he would have. He was the responsible young man who baby-sat their children, walked their dogs, and watered their plants while they were on vacation. The boy who had cleaned their gutters, mowed their lawns, and run their errands since he was ten.

They were sure the slick mess on the road would have made finding any trace of tire treads impossible. Not one single person in town doubted that for a minute, and if anyone hinted otherwise, people turned away and wandered off without finishing the conversation.

Come sunrise, following the accident, what remained of the peeper population had settled back into the streams and the muddy banks of the Delaware, but for the next two weeks they continued their piercing chirps after the sun went down. By the time they finally stopped, everyone in town knew the truth about Simon Gray.

Or so they believed.

On the day before the accident, a heat wave settled over Bellehaven like a cloud of steam. It all but sucked the air out of anyone who tried to take a deep breath. Some attributed special significance to its being April Fools' Day. But most simply found it odd to have eighty-five-degree temperatures in early April, shrugged, and went on about their business, although they were inclined to move at a much slower pace. Only the Delaware River, swollen with the spring runoff and freshly stocked with brook and rainbow trout, sped along at breakneck speed, spewing white foam over rocky ridges.

When the heat wave persisted through the following day, girls dug out last year's shorts and tank tops from attic trunks in preparation for school on Monday, and threw away lipsticks that had melted in their backpacks. By nightfall, people found themselves kicking off top sheets, digging window fans out of basements and attics, and wrapping ice cubes in face towels to lay across the backs of their necks. A few even turned on air conditioners, muttering about future electric bills that were sure to leave them paupers.

But the heat wasn't all that kept Simon Gray awake as he paced his airless bedroom that night, wearing only a pair of boxer shorts. He hadn't slept in two nights, and it didn't look as if he ever would again. Unlike everyone else in town, he barely noticed the temperature creeping toward ninety. He had other things on his mind.

When he slipped on a pair of khaki cargo shorts and a black T-shirt, silently sneaked out the back door, got in his car, and headed for the river, it wasn't in search of cooler air. What he sought was a few moments of peace. A rare minute or two when something or someone besides Devin McCafferty and the others didn't monopolize his thoughts.

He parked his Honda near the boat ramp and headed down to his favorite spot a few feet from the Delaware.

For the next half hour he watched the moonlight glimmer off the rush of water heading downriver, letting his mind flow along with it. People, he realized, were a lot like drops of water caught up in the spring runoff, shuttled into fast-moving streams that collided into rivers and rushed to join the ocean. If you got caught in the current there was no turning back. The only way out of that racing water was to evaporate into the night air.

Evaporate. Disappear.

He wondered what it would feel like to be as light as mist, to no longer be weighted down with a human body filled with leaden fears, in constant dread of being discovered, exposed, humiliated.

Simon turned his face toward the sky so thick with stars he could almost taste them on his tongue, metallic, like biting into aluminum foil. Moonlight glinted off his thick glasses, and anyone looking at his face would have thought his eyes had melted into two pools of pure light.

Sitting with his back against the base of a huge white pine, eyes closed, he listened to the gentle *hush-hush,* the whisper of the wind through the soft needles. For just the tiniest moment Simon thought he might float up into the night air and beyond. Until the piercing shrieks of two raccoons, probably males hell-bent on killing each other over a female, forced him to remember why he was here, why he hadn't been able to sleep.

He did not want to think about what would happen to him, to all of them, if they were caught. But then, maybe it was time he *was* caught, because he'd been fooling everyone for so long he'd started to fool himself. Simon the Eagle Scout. Simon the Responsible. Squeaky clean Simon. Hell, he was Bellehaven's very own Dudley Do-Right. Who was he kidding?

Even when he was caught stealing a computer game the previous fall from CompUSA, the manager, who turned out to be his old second-grade teacher, Mr. Grabowski—the upgraded Mr. Grabowski, ex-teacher, now a hotshot manager—had merely given him a friendly pat on the back and said, "Guess you had your head in the clouds, there, Simon." He had pointed to the box Simon had tucked inside his jacket. "I think you forgot to pay for that."

Yeah, right. Was the guy that dense?

Simon had lifted the box from its hiding place and said, "Oh, yeah. Sorry." And that was all there was to it. Later he realized that Mr. Grabowski hadn't wanted to believe Simon would stoop to stealing from his store. Simon himself still had no idea why he'd done it. It was the only thing he'd ever tried to steal in his life, and now he couldn't even remember the name of the computer game.

What was it with people anyway? Why did they trust him? Especially with their kids? Lately he'd taken to letting the kids do exactly what they wanted, eat Oreos and fistfuls of Froot Loops and Cocoa Puffs until they spun like twirling tops from all that sugar. He let them watch cartoons until their eyes popped right out of their heads. He liked to see the kids happy. It made him feel good.

When that didn't work, he would sometimes set them in their cribs or their playpens and let them cry until their throats were hoarse and their noses so clogged they could barely breathe. Their sobs brought him much too close to the edge, much too close to his own tears, tears he'd worked hard to control. That was when he would walk right out the back door, sit under the nearest tree, and wait for the silence, because he couldn't bear to listen to their cries. Because he didn't know how to take away their pain.

Simon folded his arms and tucked his hands beneath them. He stared out over the river. If those same moms had followed him around this past year, they would have been horrified. They would have locked their children in their rooms for safekeeping, kept their pets in their basement, shuttered their windows, pulled down their shades, and shunned the very sight of him. He imagined that even his own mother, if she had still been alive, would have turned away from him.

Sometimes, on nights when the sky had just begun to turn violet, and strange shadows seemed to hover along the edge of his backyard where it ran into the neighbor's field and to the cemetery beyond, Simon thought he saw his mother rising from her restful place beneath the pines, where she had been buried more than a year earlier, to shake her head in disapproval. On such nights, he would see her at the edge of the field, and if he stared long and hard enough, squinting into the thin line of muted orange on the horizon, if he blurred his vision ever so slightly, he could almost make out the disappointment on her face.

On these nights, he was convinced she knew everything he had ever done and considered him beyond redemption. On other nights, when he was willing to cut himself a little slack, he told himself such notions were childish fantasy. Still, despite this rationale, he had discovered he preferred the shadowy form of disapproval, hovering beyond the edge of his yard, to nothing at all.

It was almost midnight and Simon's eyelids felt heavy. The lack of sleep was catching up with him, and now it seemed his mind was beginning to play tricks, because suddenly tiny frogs were springing out of the weeds, leaping off rocks, and sending their shrill calls into the night. They flew into Simon's lap, landed in his hair, crawled into the pockets of his cargo shorts.

Frantic, he jumped to his feet, beating the frogs from his head, all the while trying not to step on any of them as he made a dash for his Honda. Dozens of frogs crawled over his car. Fortunately he had left the windows up. Still, the peepers clung to the windshield like tiny suction-cup toys. Simon pounded his fist at them from the inside, but they refused to budge. If he turned on the windshield wipers he could launch the peepers right into outer space. Then again, maybe not. Maybe he would end up with a windshield smeared with frog guts, making it even harder to see. Forget the windshield wipers.

The rearview mirror was useless. The entire rear window was coated with frogs. So were the side windows. The only way he could see to back out was to roll down his window and risk letting the frogs inside the car. He rolled the window down a few inches, enough to peer out, then pulled out of the parking lot, hoping that once he was away from the river the frogs would disappear. But to his amazement, they were everywhere. They rose out of neatly manicured lawns and bounced along the tops of boxwood hedges; they were all over the road. And the sound, as he drove over them—hundreds, maybe thousands—was the sound of tar bubbles popping on a sun-scorched road.

He had never seen anything like this before—not in all the years he'd lived in Bellehaven—not in his entire life.

As Simon approached the community park with its fifteen-mile-an-hour speed limit, the car continued to speed along—fast, then faster. With any luck at all, the frogs would blow right off the windshield. But they hung on. The faster Simon went, the louder the popping noises from beneath his tires. Desperate, he turned the radio up full blast to drown out the horrible sound.

As he passed the park—a perfect square surrounded on three sides by stately Victorian homes and the county courthouse on the fourth—he had the bizarre sensation of being in a dream. Maybe all this was a hallucination brought on by lack of sleep. He'd heard of such things. Or maybe the hallucination was the result of the heat.

As he squinted through a clear space of glass in between the frogs, Simon's eyes fell on the huge white oak up ahead. It was the oldest tree in the county, dating back to the Revolutionary War. A battle-scarred soldier. The road had been lovingly built to curve around its thick roots. Beneath its sprawling branches a tarnished bronze plaque proclaimed this the Liberty Tree.

But Simon and the other kids at school called it the Hanging Tree because more than two hundred years before, a drifter named Jessup Wildemere was hanged from its branches for murdering Cornelius Dobbler right in his own bed while he slept, stabbing him so many times the blood formed a pool on the floor, seeped through the crevices, and stained the ceiling of the parlor below.

Up ahead, a dark shadow seemed to rise out of the damp earth in front of the bronze plaque. The shadow shifted, grew filmier in the glare of Simon's headlights, but he could see it had a form—the shape of a man.

Simon's breath caught in his throat. He was so startled by the shifting figure in front of him, he didn't realize he was still flying along at fifty miles an hour. And when he did notice, it was too late. In his panic his foot slammed down on the gas pedal instead of the brake. The car's engine roared in response. The Honda hydroplaned over the slick surface, going so fast Simon thought the car had sprouted wings. His fear was replaced with a sense of wonder, a sense of absolute freedom. He felt himself being lifted right into the air. Like a drop of water evaporating, he was out of the river. *Yes!*

The sirens didn't wake Danny Giannetti because he hadn't yet gone to bed. He sat on the porch roof outside his bedroom window, watching in wonder as, below, thousands of peepers converged on the front lawn. If he lay on his stomach and leaned carefully over the edge, his fingers clamped on the rusting gutter guards, he could see the frogs on the steps, on the porch railing, on the pillars. Their green bodies, almost black in the moonlight, were dark splotches on the white paint.

His first thought, when the emergency siren sounded, was that the town had declared war on the frogs. He half expected to see fire trucks tear down the street, firefighters blasting holes in the blanket of frogs with their hoses, half expected a cavalcade of police cars, with sharpshooter cops hanging from the windows, firing nonstop as peepers sprang into the air, looking like clay pigeons as they leaped for their lives. But the emergency siren stopped. And the distant moan of police car and ambulance sirens didn't seem to be coming anywhere near Maple Avenue, where Danny lay on the porch roof, listening carefully.

Once in a while, if you paid close attention, Bellehaven might give up one of its secrets. Somewhere in town behind one of these closed doors, maybe a life-and-death emergency was unfolding. Or maybe a crime, a robbery, or even a murder. Danny was hopeful, beside himself with anticipation.

Sometimes, as in moments like this, he liked to think about his own small contribution to the town's hoard of secrets. He savored what he and only a few of his close friends knew, rolled it around in his mind like a smooth stone he couldn't stop rubbing between his thumb and fingers. In two and a half months he would graduate from high school. In the fall he would go to Dartmouth. So far, he had been accepted by almost every university he had applied to, and all because of Simon Gray and "the project."

The next day he had a test in English on Hemingway's *The Old Man and the Sea.* He was pleased with himself because for once he'd actually read the assigned book. He hadn't expected to. And with "the project," he certainly didn't need to. But somehow he'd gotten caught up in the old man's struggle to hold on to that stupid fish. Danny wanted him to win. The last thing he'd expected was for the trophy to be chewed to bare bones by sharks, nothing worth keeping, at least to Danny's way of thinking. Nothing left you could hold up and say, "See, this is what I caught. A marlin the size of Canada." But the fishermen in the old man's village seemed to think bringing home a bunch of bones was some big accomplishment.

Suckers, Danny thought, smiling to himself. They just didn't get it.

Danny, however, had it all figured out. You didn't actually have to *play* the game, you just had to know how to win it.

He turned on his back and slipped his hands behind his head. The stars were muted by the ground light, but he could still make out the North Star. Polaris. Never had he felt more sure his life was on course. The next day he would ace the test in English, as he had aced every test so far that year, and the two years before. He knew this because a copy of the test was, right that very minute, sitting in the top drawer of his desk.

The wood frame of the basement window scraped across Devin McCafferty's back as she slid through the narrow opening like a rabbit wiggling its way down into its warren. A piece of splintered wood from the frame snagged a strand of her dark red hair. She tugged at it while simultaneously trying to shake off the tiny frogs that were landing on her bare legs with soft thumps that both tickled and gave her the creeps. Her efforts were futile. There were too many of them. The soles of her sandals were sticky with their blood.

She flattened her palms on the top of an old oak dresser, one her mother had picked up at a yard sale two years earlier, intending to refinish it for Devin's basement bedroom but never quite getting around to it.

Devin's feet were almost through the window when the emergency siren wailed into the night. Her heart nearly stopped.

She sat on top of the dresser, holding her breath. She listened for the sounds of her family overhead, listened to hear if the sirens had awakened them, which they surely had. If she looked out the window, Kyle would probably still be standing beneath the grape arbor her father had built the past summer. If Kyle had any sense, he would hightail it out of there before her parents looked out the window to see what all the excitement was about and happened to spot him, standing there, his mouth smeared with the residue of Devin's Purple Passion lipstick.

She shifted her weight and with the bottom of her T-shirt wiped a clean spot on the grimy window. Kyle was gone.

Devin drew a long breath, eased herself down to the floor, and pulled back the curtain that separated her small space from the rest of the musty basement with its washer and dryer, stacked lawn furniture cushions, her father's workbench, scattered toys, and shelves crammed with clutter.

Her hand shook as she reached for the lamp switch. She couldn't be sure if the trembling and the frantic beating of her heart were the result of the siren, the fear of being caught, or Kyle's kisses. She decided it was most likely all three and doubted she would get much sleep that night.

She flicked on the light, which sat on the table next to her bed. Not a table, really, but a plastic milk crate turned on its end and covered with a flowered tablecloth. She kicked off her sandals and slipped out of her shorts and T-shirt. For once she welcomed the cool dampness of the basement. Outside, the air was so steamy it was like trying to breathe under water.

For the next few minutes she didn't move a muscle, just listened. Overhead all was quiet. She could hardly believe her luck.

When she was an only child of three, her parents had bought this small Cape Cod on Meadowlark Drive, right at the edge of town before you went up over a hill and found yourself in the middle of dairy farm country, surrounded by cornfields and cows. On muggy spring nights like this one, the smell of fertilizer hung in the air and made you gag. And you had to choose between the stench or closing your window and sweltering to death.

For years her mother kept calling the Cape Cod their starter home, even after Devin's brothers and sisters were born. But instead of moving, her father finished off the attic so the four boys could have a room of their own. Devin shared her cramped room with her two sisters. When her father built another room off the downstairs, Devin, who was by then fourteen, thought she might actually have a room of her own. And it had almost happened. But then Granddad McCafferty had a stroke and he and Devin's grandmother came to live with them, taking the new room. That was when Devin realized this was how it was going to be until the day she moved out. So she went to work converting one small corner of the basement into her own private space.

No one, least of all her parents, called it a starter home anymore. It was just plain home, a place with scarcely enough air for everyone to take a breath at the same time.

Three years before, she had begun her countdown to freedom. Every day she crossed off another square on her calendar with a red felt-tip pen. In the fall she would go to either Cornell or Middlebury, although she hadn't heard from either yet. She would live in a dorm and maybe even get an apartment of her own eventually. A whole apartment all to herself. Three years earlier she wouldn't have dreamed of getting into a good school. The best she could have hoped for was the local community college.

But all that had changed. Thanks to Simon Gray.

Kyle Byrnes barely noticed the wave of frogs washing over his feet or the blood staining the soles of his sneakers, any more than he paid attention to the blaring emergency siren as he walked down Meadowlark Drive toward his house, three blocks away. He had other concerns. Not Devin, although the warmth of her lips on his still lingered. No, this was something else entirely, something that threatened them both.

On Thursday afternoon he had overheard Dr. Schroder, the principal of Bellehaven High, telling George McCabe, the computer science teacher, that she thought someone might be hacking into the school's computer network.

Kyle had come to the computer lab to do some extra-credit work and had found the door closed. Ordinarily he would have walked right in. But as his fingers touched the knob, he thought he heard Principal Schroder's voice. She sounded upset.

Fortunately no one was in the hallway. Kyle edged closer to the door, staying long enough to hear how a copy of an English test had turned up in Angela Beckett's printer that morning. Angela Beckett was Dr. Schroder's administrative assistant. Apparently the test had been intended for another destination, another printer. George McCabe had sounded unconcerned, claiming the test probably belonged to Abel Dodge, the English teacher. "Abel sent it to the wrong printer, that's all," he assured Dr. Schroder. But the principal had countered with "I already talked to Abel. He has no idea how that test ended up in Angela's printer. And I might add, he's quite upset about it."

Dr. Schroder thought they should notify the local police, but George McCabe, who also served as the school's systems administrator, seemed to downplay the whole thing, saying it sounded like a tempest in a teapot to him. He said he would check the log on the server to see if there was anything suspicious. But Kyle could tell that Principal Schroder wanted more. "If it's a hacker," she told him, "it's a criminal offense. This is a police matter."

"I doubt it's a hacker," George McCabe told her. "It sounds like one of the students got hold of Abel's password."

"Which is a breach of security," Principal Schroder said.

It was clear to Kyle that it would be only a matter of time before there was an investigation. He'd called Simon the moment he got home from school and the two of them had met down by the river, near the boat ramp. The only thing Simon said, when Kyle finished his story, was "Well, I guess it's over." He had looked relieved, which irritated Kyle.

It *wasn't* over. Not by a long shot. Kyle wasn't about to let any of them get caught. Friday morning he and Simon skipped first period and began damage control. Simon started by removing an incriminating program he had installed in one of the library's computers, then moved on to the others. They had acted fast. Simon missed most of his morning classes but told Kyle he was pretty sure no one would be able to trace what they'd been up to.

So far, Kyle hadn't said a word to Devin or Danny. He didn't want to alarm them. They might panic and do something stupid, like blurt out everything to their parents. Especially Devin. She had a tendency to overreact. He couldn't risk that. Besides, if something came up, Simon would handle it. That was what Kyle was thinking when he turned the corner onto Edgewood Avenue and saw the whirling lights blinking on the tree branches like red strobes.

Two police cars and an ambulance were already at the scene. A crowd of people—some in bathrobes, some half dressed—stood a few yards away, kept at a distance by the police.

As Kyle neared the site of the accident, drawn like the others by morbid curiosity, he saw that a car had smashed into the Liberty Tree. He came up beside a bald man with a grizzly beard, who wore only a pair of khaki shorts.

"Looks bad," the man said, folding his arms across his hairy belly. He did not take his eyes from the car. When Kyle followed the man's gaze, his breath caught in his throat. He recognized the car. It was Simon Gray's Honda. He was certain of it. The passenger side of the front end was crushed like an aluminum can.

He pushed forward, ignoring the police officer's warnings. "I know him," Kyle shouted at the cop. "I know that kid."

The police officer dismissed Kyle's outburst with a few nods, calmly gripped Kyle's upper arm, and steered him back into the crowd, just as the paramedics lifted the gurney into the back of the ambulance. Simon's face was covered with blood; the white sheets on the gurney were soaked in red.

Kyle couldn't believe what he was seeing. This was Simon. This was someone he knew. "Is he dead?" Kyle grabbed the cop's shoulder.

The police officer patted Kyle's hand, then gently lifted it off. "Your friend's still alive," he said. "Unconscious, but there's still a pulse." He shook his head and nodded toward the crushed Honda. "That's one hell of a lucky kid, I'd say."

Kyle's mouth was so dry he could barely swallow. The scent of Simon's blood seemed to be hovering in the air. Kyle could almost taste it.

It wasn't until after the ambulance headed down Edgewood that Kyle realized his situation. Anything that Simon had left undone, any evidence left behind, any tracks they hadn't covered, would be Kyle's responsibility. And he had no idea what to do next.

Chapter 2

A few hours past sunrise a murder of crows, thousands of them, blackened the skies of Bellehaven, swooping overhead in ominous waves, barking their deafening caws. They covered the roads like fresh asphalt, devouring the dead frogs. They blanketed stream banks, their sharp beaks plucking shrieking peepers from beneath rocks.

People stood at their windows, terrified to go outside. Mothers unpacked their children's lunches and told them to go back to bed. They weren't about to risk sending them into this black blizzard.

When the phone call came, in the midst of all this chaos, Danny Giannetti was in the shower, filling the room with steam, losing himself in a mist so thick he couldn't see his hand rubbing the bar of soap along his other arm. He had no idea Bellehaven was under siege.

The rap of knuckles against the bathroom door startled him. The bar of soap thudded to the bottom of the tub.

"Phone," his sister, Marni, yelled, jiggling the knob to see if the door was locked. She stood barefoot with her head bent close to the door, listening as she zipped up her jeans. She was two years older than Danny and had a full-time job as a mechanic at the Gulf station in town. A fine line of stubborn grease was always ground into her cuticles.

"Take a message," Danny yelled.

"I'm not your damn secretary," Marni screamed back, then headed down the hall to finish getting dressed.

The sliding glass door on the shower thumped against the wall as he slammed it open, wrapped a towel around his waist, and still dripping, padded down the hallway, leaving wet footprints on the carpet.

"Yeah?" Danny barked into the phone.

"He smeared his Honda all over the Hanging Tree."

The voice belonged to Kyle Byrnes. Danny knew the voice as well as his own, had known it since kindergarten.

"Who?"

"Gray."

There was a moment of silence as Danny balanced the phone between his chin and his shoulder while he tightened the towel before it could slide from his hips. "What are you talking about?"

"The accident last night. I saw it."

When Danny didn't respond, Kyle's tone sharpened. "Did you hear what I said?"

"You saw it?"

"Yeah, on my way home from Devin's."

"Are you sure it was Gray?"

"It was Gray. I saw them loading him into the ambulance."

"Is he dead?"

"I don't know. I don't think so. Listen, we've—"

"Drunk? Was he drunk, do you think?" Danny was having trouble focusing. Simon must have walked past that tree on his way home from school every day since kindergarten, must have driven by it a hundred times since he'd gotten his license two months earlier. Everybody in town knew that the road curved around the Hanging Tree. And for those unfamiliar with the area, there were yellow signs with black arrows to guide them around the danger zone. Nobody in their right mind could possibly run into it.

"Simon Gray drunk? You're kidding, right?"

"Then why?"

"Who knows." Kyle paused to take a breath. "We've got ourselves a little problem."

"You mean Simon?"

"Something else."

"Yeah? What's that?"

"Not on the phone," Kyle said.

"Is this about the project?"

"Later."

Danny was starting to get nervous. It wasn't like Kyle

to be so cryptic. "Right. Later." Danny slammed the phone into the cradle. The news about Simon had left him badly shaken. He flattened his palms against the wall in front of him for balance.

When he got back to his room, his head felt so light he thought he might keel over. He told himself it was probably because of the hot steam in the shower. He flopped on the bed, lying on his back, and waited for the whirlpool in his head to wind down while his heart continued to bang against his chest. According to the digital clock on the nightstand, it was almost seven-thirty. He had fifteen minutes to get to school before the last bell. He couldn't afford any black marks on his record right now. The previous Thursday, after an agonizingly long wait, he had received his acceptance letter from Dartmouth, and his feet hadn't touched the ground since. Not until now. Not until Kyle's phone call.

He closed his eyes and waited for the pounding in his chest to slow down. What if Simon died? What if he had left behind any evidence?

No, not Simon. Not a chance.

Had it been only a year since he and Kyle Byrnes first cornered Simon in the cafeteria as he was dropping off his tray?

Danny remembered how they'd flanked him, walked him down the hall, straight into the custodian's closet, and pulled the chain overhead to turn on the single dim lightbulb. Surrounded by industrial-sized bottles of disinfectant, cans of Comet, boxes of sponges, and bundles of paper towels and toilet paper, they had held a brief meeting. They were juniors back then; Simon, a lowly sophomore.

Danny remembered how, in spite of Simon's small stature—five and a half feet of skin and bones—and his face, so pale he almost blended in with the wall, he had stared them right in the eye, his expression as stoic as a moose facing down an eighteen-wheeler. He didn't so much as blink. He just stood there waiting.

It was Kyle who had spoken first, Kyle with his smooth easygoing style, his friendly grin, who towered over Simon by half a foot, wearing a Tommy Hilfiger rugby shirt, as colorful and approachable as Simon's black T-shirt was darkly impenetrable. Kyle's dark hair was short and neat. Simon's, pale and shaggy, jutted out in all directions, as if he'd forgotten to comb it that morning. Face to face, they were a study in contrasts.

Kyle had been rambling on about how Simon was a living legend at Bellehaven High, how everyone knew he was a genius with computers. That was when Simon finally blinked, although his face still showed no expression. Kyle kept pouring it on. He kept it up until Simon glanced over at Danny and said, his voice flat and noncommittal, "Does this have anything to do with Walter Tate's family moving to Seattle?"

Bingo.

Danny was impressed. Simon had nailed it. He wondered if Simon knew that Walter, who'd been part of their posse since Walter was a freshman, was a vital part of the academic hub they'd created. Probably not. And neither Danny nor Kyle was about to tell him that. Not yet. It was too risky.

"Why d'you think that?" Danny asked.

Simon stuffed his hands in his jeans pockets and leaned back against the metal shelves. "Walter was in my advanced placement computer science class."

Kyle looked down at his watch. "I'm going to be late for calculus." He rested one hand on the doorknob, the other on Simon's shoulder. "Rob Fisher's having a party Saturday night. You want to come with us?"

Danny could tell by the look on Simon's face he was suspicious. He didn't trust them for a second. And why should he? They were about to sucker him into taking over Walter's place.

Within a week Simon Gray was putty in their hands.

School was the last place Danny wanted to be that morning, but he knew he had to go. So did the others. They didn't have a choice.

Danny rolled off the bed, pulled a pair of boxers from his top drawer, jammed his legs into cargo pants, yanked a navy T-shirt over his wet hair, and grabbed a cotton shirt from the closet. Usually he spent several minutes working on his hair to get it just right—short dark spikes, tipped platinum blond, carefully arranged to strike a balance somewhere between casual unkemptness and studied artifice. That morning, without even bothering to look in the mirror, he hardly took time to whip the comb across the top of his head.

Danny was halfway down the front walk when he noticed that the bare tree branches were choked with crows, crows in every tree in his yard, and in the McAllisters' yard next door, and every yard all the way down the block, for as far as he could see. Even worse, the birds had left their calling cards all over his black Mustang. Danny shook his fist at them, flipped them his middle finger, and shouted an obscenity as he climbed behind the wheel. He didn't have time for this right now. If he didn't get a move on, he'd be late. But even with all he had on his mind, he couldn't shake the eerie feeling that the birds were laughing their heads off at him as he peeled out of the driveway.

Two minutes later, just as the first bell rang, he pulled into a parking lot cluttered with crows. He wondered if they'd followed him there, then decided he was getting paranoid. The birds lined the roof of the school, rows of feathered soldiers in shiny black uniforms awaiting orders. They sent up a raucous cry as Danny headed for the front steps.

He slipped his shades from his shirt pocket, although he didn't think for a second they would be much help protecting his eyes if the birds attacked. Crows always went after their enemies in groups. Outright mobbed them. They'd even been known to eat their own, if they found them already dead. That much he knew.

Right now he was quaking in his Nikes. He'd had a horror of birds, any kind of birds, ever since he'd read the story of Prometheus in seventh grade, read how he was bound to the rocky peak of the Caucasus, where each day an eagle pecked away at his liver. And all because he stole fire from Mount Olympus and gave it to mankind. That was what happened when you pissed off Zeus, or any of the gods, back in those days. If they didn't like what you were doing, they made sure you knew.

Danny stood there, one hand hovering above his sunglasses, a visor protecting his eyes in case of an attack. He studied the crows, trying to calculate how fast he could make it to the front doors.

From somewhere behind him, he heard, "Hey, Giannetti, wait up." He didn't have to look to know it was Kyle.

He jogged up to Danny's side, a living ad for J.Crew in his khaki chinos and blue shirt. An olive green backpack hung from one shoulder. He didn't seem at all bothered by the crows. In fact, he didn't even seem to notice them. "My house. After school, okay?"

"I've got track."

"Skip it. This is important."

Danny nodded. He knew Kyle would never ask him to miss practice unless something serious was going on.

Feeling less intimidated now that reinforcements had arrived, Danny took the concrete steps two at a time, yanked open the door, and headed down the hall. Kyle was right on his heels. He clamped his hand on Danny's shoulder just as Danny was about to walk into homeroom. Danny was instantly reminded of that day in the custodian's closet, Kyle with his hand on Simon's shoulder, looking as friendly as the local Good Humor man. "Loosen up," Kyle said. "I doubt Gray's doing a whole lot of talking right now."

Danny glanced away, bothered by the look in Kyle's eyes. There was nothing Danny could say. He nodded again and slipped through the door into the classroom. But the weight of Kyle's hand on his shoulder would stay with him for the rest of the morning.

In homeroom Liz Shapiro was frantically trying to finish the last few problems of her math homework when Principal Schroder's voice crackled through the static over the PA system. It filled the room. The voice announced that Simon Gray had been in a car accident, was in a coma, would need their prayers.

Liz wanted to stand up and scream right back at the speaker above the door that it was a big lie. Simon Gray lived two doors down from her. He was her closest friend. She knew him. He was a *good* driver. A *careful* driver. A *responsible* person. Instead, she stared, silent and unmoving, at the back of Kevin Zimmerman's head, at his girlfriend's initials, S.C., cleanly shaved into his partial buzz cut, the tips of the letters slightly hidden by the longer hair growing on top of his head. She had seen this sight every morning for most of her junior year and couldn't have cared less if Kevin Zimmerman let Sara Cohen shave her initials on his head three times a week. But today it seemed important to understand why.

If Simon let her, would she put her initials on him, like personal property? Like sewing a name tag on gym shorts, or on clothes you took to camp? That was pure fantasy and she knew it. Simon was her best friend, had been since they were both in Pampers. She could not recall a time when he hadn't been a part of her life.

Liz's face grew damp with sweat as she realized too late she was about to vomit. She lunged for the door, ignoring Mr. Prendergast's protests from the front of the room, making it halfway down the hall before she threw up. The locker felt icy cold against her sweaty clothes as she slid to the floor. Her cheek rested against the cool metal. The pool of vomit was only inches from the tips of her fingers. Her head throbbed as her mind screamed over and over, Please, God, not Simon.

Saturday afternoon—only two days before—they had been sitting on the dark green couch in her family room, watching a rented video of *Forbidden Planet*. The two of them were crazy about old movies. And this was one of Simon's favorites. It had been the first day of the April heat wave and the air in the room was stifling, although every window in the house was open.

Liz was supposed to be working on a project her history teacher, Mrs. Rosen, had assigned the second day of the marking period, back in February. Everyone in the class had to select an event in American history—either local, regional, or national—and find evidence to show discrepancies or distortions in present-day accounts, evidence that, when shared with the class—everyone had to present their findings in both a written and an oral report—might change their perception of the event. "History," Mrs. Rosen had explained as she gazed out at them over the tops of her half-moon glasses, "is subjective. But there is a central truth at the core of every event. I want you to come as close to finding that truth as possible." And that, she had told the class, was their goal.

The paper was due at the end of the marking period, less than two weeks away, and would make up a third of their grades. Liz had chosen the hanging of Jessup Wildemere as her topic. It had seemed like a good idea at the time. Local legend. A bloody murder. Intriguing subject. She'd spent a few weeks on it but had become discouraged when she couldn't find much that was new or interesting.

Even though the paper loomed in the back of her mind like a dark shadow, Liz tried not to think about it. She was in a silly mood and couldn't resist making fun of the film. That was what the two of them usually did when they watched these old movies. But on this day Simon wasn't playing, and Liz could tell by the odd expression on his face that he had something on his mind. He hadn't even teased her about her hair, which in a fit of PMS frenzy she'd taken a pair of scissors to the day before, hacking her long dark tresses into short uneven layers. She left the results tangled and uncombed, as if she'd just rolled out of bed. And truth be told, she was rather pleased with the results. But Simon didn't even notice.

Then, as if they'd never been watching the movie at all, as if they were picking up where they'd left off with some other conversation that Liz couldn't remember, a conversation that perhaps Simon had been having in his own mind, he said, "I'm thinking about going out West and getting a job next year."

This was such a startling revelation that Liz bolted upright. She hit the Pause button on the remote and slid to the edge of the couch. "You mean drop out?" She couldn't believe what she was hearing. Simon had always been at the top of his class. He was brilliant with computers, with anything to do with technology. Everyone, including Liz, assumed next November he'd be applying for early acceptance to MIT or Carnegie Mellon.

"Maybe."

"And what, go out West? You mean like wearing a Stetson and going on cattle drives?" It was a ludicrous picture and they both knew it.

The old Simon would have laughed. The Simon who had been hers long before Kyle and his friends took over his life. But now he sat there staring at the frozen TV screen and never even cracked a smile, as if he hadn't heard her, didn't even know she was still in the room.

Liz reached over and tapped him on the head. "Hello in there." She leaned forward, tilting her head to get a better look at his eyes, eyes the color of the sea—a dark and stormy sea. And that startled her. She stared at him, as if trying to see right inside his head. Because sometimes that worked. Sometimes she could almost read Simon's thoughts. They had known each other *that* long.

Simon stood up so suddenly he had to grab the back of the couch for balance. "I've got to get home," he said. He crossed the room to the French doors that led out to the patio.

"Something's wrong, isn't it?" Liz prodded. "I mean, *really* wrong."

Simon gripped the doorknob. "Nothing's wrong." His voice was flat.

"The smartest kid in Bellehaven High wants to drop out of school and that's not something wrong?"

Simon stared across the room at her. For a few hopeful seconds she thought he was going to tell her what was really on his mind, when suddenly the movie roared into the awkward silence. Instead of hitting the Pause button again, Liz turned off the TV.

"Maybe I don't want to go to college. Maybe it's that simple," he said.

Liz began nervously twisting a jagged strand of hair. It wasn't "that simple" at all, and she knew it. But she wasn't sure how to get Simon to talk about what was bothering him. And in the end, she said exactly the wrong thing. "There's more to it than that," she said. "I know you, Simon."

He yanked open the door and looked over at her. His eyes were hooded, unreadable. "You don't know me at all. You just like to think you do."

Liz felt as if he'd given her a karate chop across her windpipe. For the first time in their friendship, she didn't have a clue what was going on in Simon's mind. And now it appeared as if she never had. So she let him go. Let him walk right out the door.

Now he was in the hospital, in a coma, and might never come back to her.

Someone had grabbed Liz by the elbow and was attempting to help her up. She stared up into the puffy red face of Mr. Prendergast. His tie flopped awkwardly against the top of her head as he struggled to get her to her feet. Liz was all too aware that she was a little overweight, that the size ten jeans she'd bought a few months ago were getting difficult to zip up, but Prendergast's grunting made her feel like a whale. She shoved him away. "I'm fine," she said, scrambling to her feet.

Mr. Prendergast had already called Clyde Zukowski, the custodian, who showed up with a bucket of disinfectant and a mop. He scratched the white stubble on his pockmarked face and glared at Liz as if she were Typhoid Mary, carrying some insidious disease that might wipe out the entire school population if he didn't get this mess cleaned up fast.

Before the first-period bell rang, Mr. Prendergast had written Liz a hall pass, handed her her backpack, and sent her off to the nurse. But Liz walked right past the door of the nurse's room, ducked below the glass window of the main office so Angela Beckett, the principal's administrative assistant, couldn't see her, and slipped out the front door of the school. She was going to the hospital. And she was going to pull Simon out of this coma if it took every last ounce of will she had.

The clock above the waiting room door ticked toward eight-thirty. If she had been in school that morning, which wasn't going to happen, Courtney Gray would have been facing a history test. This was the only good thing that could be said for the moment. She was here, in the hospital, and would not be sweating bullets over Mr. Meehan's exam in first period.

Her father was in the intensive care unit with Simon. She and her father had been at the hospital since twelve-thirty in the morning, after driving through a nightmarish plague of peepers until they reached the outskirts of town, where suddenly, miraculously, the roads were clear again. The flood of frogs, their incessant chirping, like an onslaught of half-crazed, half-starved baby chicks, had made the journey to the hospital seem all the more surreal. Still, she would have traded this real world, where her brother lay broken and bruised, for that unreal world, frogs and all, in a heartbeat.

Standing by the foot of his bed, Courtney had stared down at her brother's battered face. Lips that didn't twitch, eyelids that never fluttered. A bruised, swollen face. A body full of tubes. Clear plastic hoses of various sizes running up his nose, into his mouth, and into his arm, all hooked up to an array of intimidating machines: a respirator to keep him breathing, a monitor with its colored lines bleeping across the screen to let everyone know Simon was still among the living—although barely—and bags of dripping fluids that hung on the IV pole. She was allowed only ten minutes with him, although she had left the room before her visiting time was up, left because she couldn't stand it another minute. She had headed straight for the waiting room around the corner from the entrance to the intensive care unit.

There were two waiting rooms, side by side. In the larger room were a TV and a table with a coffee machine. Courtney would have preferred this to the other room, which was not much bigger than a walk-in closet and held only six chairs. But a man and two boys were in the larger room, watching cartoons. She was in no mood for the Road Runner.

She had tried the main waiting room across from the cafeteria. It was large and bright, but the huge sprawling palms reminded her of something out of *Little Shop of Horrors,* and to make matters worse, a woman with three small children was leading her kids in some song-and-dance routine. Courtney thought if she heard the woman sing, "If you're happy and you know it, clap your hands," one more time, she'd have to swat her with a rolled-up magazine.

In desperation, she had returned to the cramped, cheerless room with six chairs, all upholstered in a faded beige fabric and soiled with stains.

Someone was paging Dr. Greenberg. The woman's voice echoed over the PA system, rumbled like a bowling ball down the hallway. Courtney held her breath. Dr. Greenberg was Simon's doctor.

For just the briefest moment Courtney thought about going back to the ICU to find out why the nurse was paging Dr. Greenberg. But for some reason her body didn't want to cooperate. She couldn't seem to make herself get up. She'd had about enough of this. She wanted to go home. *Now.* And she wanted to take Simon with her.

Instead, she stared down at her hands, ignoring the red raw rims around her cuticles, so that she didn't have to look at the hospital's mission statement—the only thing mounted on the bare walls—for the thousandth time. She noticed a spot of tomato sauce the size of a fifty-cent piece on her T-shirt, right above the blue bird made of sequins. She ran her hand through her spiky blond hair, realizing as her fingers became tangled that she'd never bothered to comb it before they left the house. She hoped no one she knew showed up. She looked like hell.

This was all her father's fault. If he hadn't been standing in the doorway of her bedroom barking orders at her, as he always did, yelling for her to "get a move on," Courtney would have had time to pick out something decent to wear instead of grabbing wrinkled jeans and a stained T-shirt from the pile of dirty clothes on her floor.

Right now she wished she had brought a sweater. The hospital was cold enough to give her frostbite, even though it was eighty degrees outside and the air was so heavy you could drown in it.

Courtney reached for a magazine, opened it, and laid it against her chest to hide the tomato-sauce stain. She slid down in her chair, crossed her legs at the ankles, and leaned her head against the wall, right over someone else's oily stain. Fragments of history—facts temporarily wedged into her brain from cramming the night before—skipped through her mind at random. She tried to second-guess the questions Mr. Meehan would have on the test. What is the Emancipation Proclamation? In what year did Lincoln deliver the Gettysburg Address? Give three reasons why the country went to war. They had been studying the Civil War this marking period. Right now it was a whole lot easier to think about a war that had torn apart the nation than about her brother.

Although she would never admit it to anyone, sometimes Courtney thought Simon was all that stood between her and the loony bin. He was the buffer between her and their father. Her father drove her nuts. He was always on her case about something these days. She spent a good deal of her energy finding ways to avoid him.

The past Thursday, two days before the heat wave struck, Simon had come across her smoking pot behind the garage by the woodpile. He stood there with his hands in his sweatshirt jacket, looking more like one of her freshman friends than a high school junior. But he didn't freak out or anything when he saw her. Not like their dad would have. Instead he sat down on the ground next to her, leaned back against the garage wall, and stared up at the overcast sky.

Courtney's instinct was to squash the joint into the mud and claim it was only a bidi, mango flavored, not even a real cigarette. But she didn't want to waste good pot. Instead she kept her gaze aimed straight ahead, as if she hadn't even noticed Simon.

Beyond their backyard was an open field, and beyond that, the cemetery where their mother was buried. A large sycamore spread its bony arms above some of the headstones as if it wanted to gather them all up in one swoop. It was too early for leaves, although buds had begun to appear.

When the joint was too small to hold anymore, Courtney squeezed the lit end with her thumb and forefinger in short, quick nips, then put the roach in her pocket.

With his eyes on the distant headstones, Simon asked, "Does it help?"

No one but Simon could know what it was like living with their father since their mother had died. It was like living with a human land mine—the slightest little thing could set him off. And no one but Simon would understand why she was smoking pot. "Yeah. It does." Courtney dug her fingers into her scalp and rubbed the top of her head violently, as if she were trying to trench through to her brain. "Sometimes."

Simon nodded but didn't say anything more. That drove Courtney nuts.

When she wanted to get on his nerves, she called him Simon the Good or Saint Simon. For as long as she could remember, he'd never gotten in trouble for anything. Nothing serious, anyway. It wasn't normal. "It's not like I'm addicted, you know. I've only tried it a couple times."

When Simon didn't respond, Courtney turned to him with a thin half smile. "Like you don't have any escape hatches." She lifted a rock by her thigh, bounced it up and down on her palm a few times, then flung it into the open field. It made a dull thud as it landed in the damp earth. "You want to talk about addictions? What about all the time you spend at the computer? I can't even get near it. Not even when I've got a paper to write."

"Who said I wanted to talk about addictions?" A cold wind seemed to rise out of nowhere, setting the sycamore branches flailing in a frantic motion and rustling the cornstalk stubble in the open field. Simon pulled the hood of his sweatshirt up over his head.

Courtney thought he looked like a monk.

She knew he wouldn't argue with her. Not like he used to. He never even teased her anymore. Not since their mother had died a year ago from a staph infection after a routine appendectomy. Nobody had seen it coming. It just happened. One minute she was fine, excited about coming home the following day, and three days later she was gone.

That was why Courtney hated hospitals, hated doctors, hated nurses. She didn't trust them. But most of all, she hated being there, in that place, waiting to see if they were going to screw up on Simon too.

Chapter 3

IT WAS NOT UNUSUAL FOR PEOPLE WHO WERE OUT for a Sunday drive, weaving down narrow country roads past dairy farms and fields of corn, to suddenly stumble upon the town of Bellehaven. Expecting to find a continuous expanse of fields and farms, they were rarely prepared for what met their gaze when they crested the steep hill and found, spread out below—as if it had materialized out of thin air like the mythical town of Brigadoon—Bellehaven, with all its Victorian homes nestled among ancient oaks and maples, hidden where no one could ever find it unless they wanted to, or unless they just happened upon the town by accident. If you weren't expecting anything to be there, the very sight of it could take your breath away, especially in the spring when all of Edgewood Avenue was shimmering with crabapple blossoms.

It was still too early for blossoms, although the unusually warm weather had teased little buds from the branches.

Four blocks from Edgewood, Kyle Byrnes stood at the front window in the living room of the narrow Victorian where he lived with his mother, watching for Danny and Devin. His mother, a court stenographer, was at the courthouse and wouldn't be home until sometime after five. His father, last they heard, was working as a short-order cook at some grill in Connecticut.

Kyle spotted Devin as she turned the corner. She stopped to shift her backpack to her other shoulder. She had the most graceful way of walking Kyle had ever seen, even with the weight of the backpack tugging awkwardly at her shoulder.

The night before, they had been making out in an old deserted shack down by the Manunkachunk River that ran through town. The night before that, they had gone to a movie in Hackettstown. And not once, during all that time together, had Kyle mentioned the conversation he'd overheard between Dr. Schroder and Mr. McCabe on Friday. He dreaded hysterics. And he was pretty certain Devin would go ballistic when she heard. Right now he was thanking his lucky stars none of the other kids they hung out with were in on "the project," that they'd never even known about it. It was going to be hard enough dealing with Danny and Devin.

Danny pulled up in his Mustang just as Devin reached

the front walk. Kyle handed them both cans of Pepsi when they came through the front door, not even bothering to ask, and popped one open for himself.

All of them were supposed to be someplace else. Kyle, the senior class president, had a student council meeting he'd had to cancel. Devin, who had the role of Lady Macbeth in the school play, should have been at rehearsal. Danny was supposed to be at track. Only Kyle knew how important this meeting was, knew they needed to figure out a way to keep the lid on things. Otherwise all hell was going to break loose.

Devin dropped her backpack by the coffee table and curled into the corner of the couch. The temperature had been climbing all day and had finally hit eighty-seven. The room felt like a steam bath. She rolled her thick hair into a French twist, reached into her pocket for her claw clip, realized it was in her backpack, and leaned her head against the back of the couch to keep her hair off her sweaty neck. "I don't see why we had to meet right after school," she told them. "I could get replaced by my understudy if I'm not careful."

Danny eased into the recliner by the fireplace and pulled the tab on his can of soda. "Simon's in a coma and you're worried about a stupid play?"

"That's not what I meant. I feel horrible about what's happened to Simon." Devin looked over at Kyle and with her eyes signaled him to help her out. "I just don't see why we couldn't have met later."

"We're all worried about Simon," Kyle said. "But we've got other problems."

Danny took a swallow of Pepsi. "Yeah, for starters we don't have a clue what the guy's got on his PC at home. He used it to log on to the school server a few times. What if that kid sister of his uses his computer? There could be all kinds of evidence—e-mails, chat room stuff—it's all traceable."

"It's more complicated than that," Kyle said. He was standing by the window looking out at the front walk as if expecting someone else to show up.

"Why would anyone even bother with Simon's PC?" Devin said. "It's not like anyone knows what's been going on, it's not—" She paused midsentence. Kyle had turned away from the window and was looking straight at her. "What?"

While Danny and Devin listened with growing alarm, Kyle told them about the conversation he'd overheard between Dr. Schroder and Mr. McCabe, about the discovery of the English test and the possible investigation.

Danny shook his head, as if he couldn't quite believe what he was hearing. "We're screwed."

Devin glared at Kyle. "You've known about this since Friday and you didn't tell us? I spent half my weekend with you. Why didn't you tell me?"

"Did Simon know?" Danny asked.

"Simon was the first person I told," Kyle said. "I called him from the school. We had to move fast. Damage control. He's already removed the recorder program from the library computer and the two in the computer lab. There's no evidence that we ever used it."

"I can't believe you didn't tell me," Devin said.

"Hey, it's not like you were the only one left out of the loop," Danny told her. The palms of his hands were growing damp with prickly sweat. He was only now beginning to realize he'd made a mistake. A huge mistake. When his first effort to print out his English test the previous Thursday had failed, he'd tried again, selecting a different printer. This time successfully. It never once occurred to him that his initial aborted attempt might have survived somewhere else in the system, printed out to someone else's printer. He realized now that he should have known better.

Devin rolled her eyes. She leaned forward, holding her head in her hands. "You *guys* . . . this is serious. How did that test end up in the secretary's printer, anyway? Who's got Abel Dodge's English class?"

She looked at Kyle, who shrugged. She and Kyle were in the same English class, and it wasn't Abel Dodge's. They both turned to Danny. "It was you, wasn't it?" Devin said. "You're the one who printed out the English test to the wrong printer."

"Hey, how was I supposed to know where the damn test was going to end up? It was an accident. It wouldn't have happened if Simon hadn't bolted on me before the job was done."

"Meaning what?" Devin said. Her chest was so tight she could barely take a breath. She was just now remembering that Simon had promised to come to her rehearsal after school last Thursday.

Danny shrugged. "He had to meet someone. Like you'd have thought it was the President or something.

Like he couldn't wait five more minutes for me to print out the test?"

"So you printed it out yourself after he'd found the file for you?" Devin said.

"Well, yeah. Why not? I told him I could do it myself. No biggie."

"Apparently," Devin said, clenching her teeth, "you were wrong about that. God, what a moron."

"It's done, okay?" Kyle said, breaking into the conversation. "Blaming Danny or Simon or anyone at this point is a waste of time." He rubbed his eyes, trying to collect his thoughts. "They know someone's gotten into the system. They know it was the English test they were after. They'll be looking for anything suspicious." He turned to Danny. "When's your test?"

"You mean, when *was* it?"

"You already took it?" Devin shook her head. "Oh, god. It's over."

"What? I ace all my tests," Danny said. "They're not going to suspect me. They'll be looking for some kid who usually screws up and suddenly pulls an A plus." He was on his feet, pacing in front of the fireplace. "If I flunked the exam it would look a hell of a lot more suspicious. I've been acing most of my tests since I was a sophomore. They think I'm a frigging genius. If I'd suddenly blown this one, it'd send up red flags for sure."

"He's right," Kyle conceded. "We can't do anything to call attention to ourselves."

"Oh, really?" Devin said. "Have you considered how

we're all going to get through the rest of senior year without messing up?"

"Two and a half months till graduation," Danny said. "We can chalk it up to senioritis. We all got into the schools we wanted."

Devin ignored this last remark. Although she'd been accepted by Lafayette, she was still hoping to hear from Cornell, even though most universities had sent their acceptance letters and packets, and their denials, more than a week earlier. By now almost all the kids in Bellehaven High who had applied the past winter knew what their options were. "The admissions directors will expect us to keep our grades up," she warned. "You can't just start flunking courses and expect them to chalk it up to senioritis."

"Who said anything about flunking?" Kyle frowned at her. "We're not exactly a remedial teacher's nightmare. Who says we can't keep our grades up for the next two months? We just have to study. You can manage that, can't you?"

Devin looked away. She hated it when Kyle made her feel stupid. And she was still steaming because he hadn't told her sooner about the conversation between Schroder and McCabe.

"We're going to have to take this one day at a time," Kyle said. "For now, we do nothing. Except keep our ears open. If we see anyone new spending lots of time in the computer lab, especially after hours, that's a bad sign. If they start taking PCs out for 'repair,' also not good. We've got to find a way to ride this out. Maybe they'll never figure out what happened. There's only one person in Bellehaven High smart enough to do that."

They all nodded.

"Simon," Danny said, barely above a whisper.

With the heat wave in its third day, swarms of mosquitoes began to rise out of abandoned tires, rain barrels, and anything else that held even the smallest amount of water. But Devin McCafferty never noticed. Anyone watching her walk home that afternoon would have thought she'd had a few beers in the girls' room at school earlier instead of a Pepsi at Kyle's. They wouldn't guess that her unsteady gait was an attempt to keep from stepping on squashed peepers. Because despite the pieces of frogs ground into the asphalt, pieces so flattened even the crows couldn't pick them off the sun-soft tar, she was walking right down the middle of the road. If she walked on the sidewalk the crows—feathery black clouds of them, hovering on the branches of the elms along Meadowlark Drive—would cover her with their droppings. As it was, she was sorely tempted to carry her backpack on her head to keep anything disgusting from getting in her hair.

A few times the crows lifted into the air, giving her hope. Maybe they would leave, settle somewhere else. But to her disappointment, their frenzied fluttering lasted only a few brief seconds before they settled back onto the tree branches.

She tried to listen for oncoming cars over the noisy

birds, but she couldn't seem to concentrate. She was too upset, too preoccupied thinking about what would happen if there was an investigation at the school. What if Simon hadn't gotten rid of all the evidence? She felt guilty for worrying about her own skin when Simon lay in a coma, but she couldn't seem to help it.

Scarcely five minutes had passed since Devin had left Kyle's house. The meeting had meant missing rehearsal. She worried about losing her part, even though she wasn't thrilled with the play Mr. Newcombe, the drama coach, had chosen. She had been hoping, along with everyone else, that he would let them put on *Grease* this year. Or even *Hair.* But the man was a Shakespeare fanatic. Every year since he'd come to Bellehaven High twelve years earlier, the annual school play had been something by Shakespeare. This year it was *Macbeth.* Devin was excited about landing the lead female role, although she disliked the character. It made her uncomfortable to speak some of Lady Macbeth's lines. Not that she would have admitted this to anyone. Besides, having the lead in the school play looked good on her college applications.

The afternoon was so hot it felt more like the middle of August than early April. The air in her lungs felt like steam from a teakettle. Strands of hair were glued to her face with sweat. She wished the community pool were open. Thinking about the pool reminded her of the past summer, when she and Kyle would sneak over the chain-link fence late at night and go skinny-dipping. Lying on the soft grass, away from the telling glare of the security lights, staring up at the stars, they planned their futures between long warm kisses, Kyle talking about Harvard as if it were heaven. Now, with Simon's help, Kyle's dream had become a reality.

And today, when she got home, Devin found two thick envelopes in the mailbox, one from Cornell, her first choice, and another from Middlebury. She knew without opening them that she'd been accepted by both. Yet she felt no excitement. Not even relief. Nothing.

She sat down on the front stoop of her house, holding the envelopes in her lap. Her father's eighteen-wheeler was parked in the road by the curb. He must have gotten home from his latest run earlier than expected. Sometimes she wished he would find somewhere else to leave his truck, instead of announcing for the whole world to see that he was a truck driver. Devin knew he was proud of what he did, proud of owning his own rig, proud of being, as he often told her, "his own man." Devin wasn't proud at all. She was embarrassed. And even worse, she felt guilty for these traitorous thoughts. This was the man who had worked hard all his life to keep seven kids in shoes and to be able to take his family and his parents out to Pizza Hut once a month.

Behind her she heard her brothers and sisters and their friends shrieking and laughing as they charged around the corner of the house blasting each other with water from their Super Soakers. For just that moment she wanted to be them. Or at least to be that age again, back when her biggest worry had been whether or not she'd be able to get a chicken breast when nine forks simultaneously dove for the small plate of fried chicken in the middle of the table. Rarely did she get a breast. Usually she ended up with two wings, or maybe a leg. You had to be fast in a house with seven kids.

Devin stared down at the envelopes on her lap but couldn't bring herself to open them. These were her tickets out of here. There was no way in hell her parents would ever be able to pay for her college education. She knew that, had always known it. But she and Kyle and Danny, none of whom came from families with money, had already thought of that. The scholarships were to be part of "the project." Now, with Simon in a coma, she wondered how they were ever going to pull off this last crucial part of the plan.

Her sweaty fingers left damp prints on the envelopes. Her thoughts turned again to Simon. Simon, who had helped all of them, who had never once used his skills to improve his own academic situation, and who might be dying.

As if that weren't bad enough, there was something else. Simon was in love with her. Devin had known this from the first day he started hanging around with them, the day Kyle brought him to Rob Fisher's party. She saw how Simon couldn't keep his eyes off her. And she knew at once he was theirs, knew she'd be able to get him to do things he might not have done otherwise.

Now it was eating away at her. She could feel it in her stomach, like a sack full of baby alligators, trying to chew their way out. The only way to put an end to the incessant, painful gnawing was to go to Principal Schroder and tell her the truth. But Devin would never do that. Not to Kyle. Not to herself. And most of all, not to Simon.

Simon sat on the edge of Stanley Isaacson's bed while the old man told him about the time he was on a submarine in the Pacific. "Like being in a metal coffin," he said. And Simon knew what he meant, because that was exactly what had happened to him. Only there was no one else there with him. No submarine crew for company.

He knew what it was like to be locked inside a dark place. But sometimes he got out. He wasn't sure how he did it, only that it had happened twice so far. This was his second journey, and it had brought him to Mr. Isaacson's room, three doors down from his own. Mr. Isaacson, who had thick tufts of white hair growing from his ears but only a few thin wisps on his head, told Simon to call him Stanley. When Stanley talked about the war, about being in the sub with the lights out, feeling the rumble of depth charges only yards away, his withered body stiffened, his knobby fingers clutched at the lightweight hospital blanket. Simon thought he could smell Stanley's fear. It smelled like seaweed, dark clumps stretched out on the wet sand.

People walking past the door thought Stanley Isaacson, who was eighty-nine years old, was having a conversation with himself. They weren't in the least surprised, given his age, that he was suffering from dementia and would soon be going to a nursing home. They did not see

Simon sitting on Stanley's bed. No one could see him. Except, apparently, Stanley Isaacson.

Simon made this discovery the first time he found himself outside his body. It had taken him a few minutes to realize that the person he was staring down at in the hospital bed was himself. He could make out the shape of the nose, the swollen purple eyelids, the chin. Part of his head was hidden beneath bandages. He could tell they had shaved some of his hair, although the section was now covered in white gauze stained with yellowy-rust-colored Betadine.

He thought he should feel something—pain, sorrow, a sense of loss—but he was surprised to feel only indifference and absolute calm. He was more interested in the rhythm of the respirator and the colored lines blip-blipping across the screen of the monitor.

The air smelled of bleach. The room was dim and ice cold.

He tried to remember why he was in this place. But he couldn't. All he recalled from the night of the accident was a single, exhilarating sensation: the rush of finding himself suddenly airborne—launched like a rocket—of flying into the night, free as a bird.

A short time later, although he couldn't be sure how much time had actually passed, he had found himself outside his room, near the nurses' station, where two doctors were talking. He stood only two feet from them, but neither seemed to notice him. Simon knew what it was like to be in a room full of people and not have anyone notice you, what it was to feel like a chameleon, taking on the color, any color, of the wall behind you, to have people almost knock you over in the hall between classes and never acknowledge the physical connection. He thought about these things and realized his present situation wasn't all that different.

He tried waving his hands over his head to get their attention, but the doctors never so much as glanced his way. They couldn't see him. That was when Simon realized he must be dead.

And he would have gone right on thinking that, if one of the doctors hadn't headed back toward Simon's room. Within seconds Simon's ears filled with a strange whooshing sound. He felt himself propelled like smoke through the stem of a pipe, right back into his body. He knew this because it was completely dark and all he could feel was pain, all he could hear was the doctor's voice hovering somewhere overhead before Simon floated off into blissful unconsciousness.

Now, sitting on the edge of Stanley Isaacson's bed, Simon wondered if maybe he could go a little farther than Stanley's room. He'd managed to come this far. Maybe he could even leave the hospital. Who would know?

When Simon got up to leave, Stanley pleaded with his eyes. Simon knew, without their speaking a word to each other, that Stanley would give anything to be able to come with him. But Simon doubted this was possible. Stanley was still burdened by his body.

As Simon passed the nurses' station, across from Stanley's room, one of the nurses was dropping two Alka-Seltzer tablets into a glass of water, waiting for them to dissolve while she looked over a list of medications she needed to dispense. She never looked up. But Simon knew that even if she had, she wouldn't have seen him.

Somehow he found his way to the lobby, although he had no memory of how he came to be there. He stood by the information desk, watching two elderly women laughing over photographs one was showing to the other. He was almost to the front door, almost out of this place, when he felt the tug, heard the whooshing sound, and knew there was nothing he could do to stop his body from pulling him back into its dark cell.

Chapter 4

The sun was setting when Liz Shapiro got off the bus out on Route 40. She had at least a mile's walk to Bellehaven since no buses came through the town, but she didn't mind. She was in no hurry to get home. Her mother would be waiting, ready to pounce the minute she walked through the door, ready to read her the riot act for being late. Who needed that?

She had spent almost the entire day at the hospital, sitting with Simon's sister, Courtney, in a cramped, depressing waiting room. She'd stayed even though no one would let her into the intensive care unit to see Simon, not even for ten seconds. Not that she hadn't tried. She'd pleaded with every nurse and doctor who came down the hall, did everything but get down on her knees.

The doctors had not expected Simon to make it through the night, although they never said so to his family. Courtney had told Liz this. She had overheard two of the nurses talking.

"They're full of it," Courtney said. "They don't know Simon."

And Liz agreed. Simon was a lot tougher than most people gave him credit for. His frail appearance was deceiving. But it scared her that the doctors had expected him to die. She could not imagine a world without Simon Gray, could not imagine getting up in the morning knowing he wouldn't be a part of her day.

When Mr. Gray came back from walking the grounds outside the hospital and found her sitting with Courtney, he told Liz to go home. He wasn't being unkind, just his usual direct self. Liz knew he didn't see any point in her being there. Her presence wouldn't change anything. Even she knew that.

Liz had stared up at his drawn, pale face, shadowed with stubble. She felt bad for him, this large bearlike man with dark hair, his coloring so completely opposite from his son's, except for the blue-gray eyes. Even Mr. Gray wasn't allowed more than ten-minute visits each hour, which was why he spent most of his time in the cafeteria drinking coffee or outside walking. But Liz stayed anyway, stayed until Mr. Gray showed up again and this time insisted she go home, saying her family would worry. He assured her that if there was any change, he'd let her know. Then he went back to Simon's room.

As Liz was getting up to leave, Courtney reached for

her hand, then quickly dropped it. "He's a real jerk sometimes," she said.

Liz looked down at her, surprised. "Who?"

Courtney shrugged. "My dad, who else?"

"He's just upset," Liz told her.

Courtney slumped in the chair, rested her elbows on the wooden arms, and linked her fingers across her stomach. "That was all bull about letting you know if anything changes."

"Maybe not." Liz swung her backpack up and slipped the strap over one shoulder. "He knows Simon and I are friends."

For the first time since Liz had showed up at the hospital, Courtney smiled at her. "Friends, huh?"

Liz was so flustered by the knowing look on Courtney's face, she couldn't think straight. Without another word she had headed for the door.

Swirling clouds of mosquitoes, like small tornadoes, spun above the marshy grass beside the road as Liz headed for home. Beyond was the Manunkachunk River, which ran right through the middle of town, joining the Delaware on the other side. Even with the sun sinking behind the trees, the evening was still muggy. Streaks of perspiration snaked down the sides of Liz's face. She shifted her backpack to redistribute the weight. She was still a good half mile from town.

When they were in elementary school, Liz and Simon often rode their bikes from town to Route 40, the only main highway that came anywhere near Bellehaven. They'd get that far and then sit on the hood of Mrs. Gray's old Buick in the parking lot of the A&P where she was a part-time checkout clerk and watch the traffic, although not many cars traveled this route anymore, not since I-80 and I-78 had been built.

As far as Liz knew, Simon hadn't set foot inside the A&P since his mother had died, more than a year earlier. He wouldn't even go near the place, as if the store had had something to do with his mother's death.

Sometimes she and Simon had taken the back way home from the A&P, just so they could come up over the hill into town. They would turn off on the road across from the deserted gas station, their feet pumping the pedals, the wind blow-drying their sweaty hair, as they flew past acres and acres of apple orchards, racing to see who could make it to the top first. In the spring the smell of the blossoms made Liz light-headed, and in the fall, the pungent odor of the apples left behind to rot on the ground almost brought tears to her eyes.

She had lived in Bellehaven all her life, yet she never failed to feel the thrill of cresting the hill and finding the town spread out below with all its houses nestled safely among the flowering trees.

Even now, as she climbed the hill, having decided to come home the back way, Liz felt that same strange sense of timelessness, of things having stood still for the people of Bellehaven. And if Simon hadn't been in the hospital in a coma, near death, she might have gone right on believing things would always be the same.

That night, as she reached the top of the hill, all she saw in the graying dusk were bony branches thick with crows. The only sounds were their caws and the shrill chirps of the peepers.

At the far end of the yard behind her house, and the other stately Victorian homes along Willowbrook Road, a stream gushed with the spring runoff. Here the chirping grew even louder. It would be like this until the frogs found their mates.

Liz walked across the backyard. The last two weeks of March had been unusually wet, with long, heavy rainfalls that had created cozy breeding grounds for early-hatching mosquitoes and left the earth soft and spongy. It felt like something living and breathing beneath Liz's feet, as if she were walking across the belly of a giant. She stood by the edge of the stream, listening. She had heard these sounds every year since the day she was born, but for the first time she realized that the noise the peepers made tonight, the high, then low chirps, repeated and repeated and repeated, had the rhythm of a heart beating. And for the first time since she'd heard the news about Simon over the PA system that morning, she began to cry.

Later, when Liz came through the back door, she found her mother sitting at the kitchen table, typing away on her laptop. Most likely, Liz decided, she was working on her latest romance novel for her mass-market publisher. Although her mother had a large office on the second floor, she claimed she did her best work at the kitchen table where fifteen years before, when Liz was only a toddler, she had written her first book on a yellow legal pad.

A nicotine patch was stuck to her mother's upper arm, and a pack of Wrigley's spearmint gum was only inches from her hand, just in case. Her mother had been trying to quit smoking for almost a year, had succeeded for months at a time, then fallen back into the old habit. This was her third try and Liz was hoping like crazy she would make it this time.

Right now Liz was fully prepared for a scene. She was, after all, late, had missed dinner, hadn't called. She was without question expecting her mother to fly into a rage. What she did not expect were her mother's arms around her, her hands stroking her hair and her voice whispering how sorry she was about Simon, and how awful about the accident. Liz was not prepared for this unexpected kindness. And just when she thought she had cried away every last ounce of water in her entire body, the tears began all over again.

Chimes echoed from somewhere deep inside a cave, becoming more and more persistent until, finally, Courtney opened her eyes. She was on the couch in the family room. She was wearing a pair of cutoffs and a T-shirt, which she'd had to dig out of the trunk of summer clothes in the attic, because it still felt like August outside.

The chiming, she now realized, was the doorbell. The early-afternoon sun coming through the windows was so bright Courtney squinted and staggered, still half asleep, toward the front hall.

Through the peephole in the door, she could see two people standing on the stoop, a man and a woman. Jehovah's Witnesses, she thought, and was about to return to the couch when she was startled by a loud knock and someone saying in a firm voice, "Police. Open up."

Suddenly she was in some old *NYPD Blue* rerun. This was a dream. It had to be. Neither the man nor the woman was wearing a uniform. Courtney's heart was racing so fast she couldn't think straight. Someone had told the police she smoked pot. Maybe someone from school. Maybe Simon. No, not Simon. "I need to see some identification," she shouted at them through the door, hoping her shaky voice didn't give her away.

Both officers flipped open black wallet-size folders and flashed IDs and a badge a few feet from the peephole.

"I'm Lieutenant Debra Santino," the woman said. "And this is Sergeant Jerry Fowler."

Satisfied, Courtney eased the door open a few inches and looked up at them with one eye. "What do you want?" she asked.

Debra Santino had short brown hair and a light dusting of freckles on her cheeks. She looked friendly enough, like somebody's mom, dressed in gray slacks and an ice blue blouse. Sergeant Fowler was more intimidating. A dark shadow of stubble covered the lower part of his face. His eyebrows were thick, almost meeting above his crooked nose, and he had a deep cleft in his chin. He wore a navy blue suit and a tie, even though rivulets of sweat were running down the sides of his face.

"I can't let anyone in the house," Courtney said. She wondered if she should mention she was home alone, that her father was at the hospital where her brother was fighting for his life. Her father had been there since the day before, only coming home long enough to drop her off early that morning in time for school. Almost thirty hours sitting in a waiting room at the hospital, and he actually expected her to go to school. If she hadn't been so upset about Simon, she would have danced the whole way from the car to the door, right in front of her obviously delusional father.

Lieutenant Santino was looking at her with large dark eyes. "I'm sorry," she said. "But we have a search warrant."

Her partner pulled a folded document from his inside coat pocket and presented it to Courtney, who stared down at it but didn't open the door an inch farther. Her stomach felt like a blender full of ice cream on high speed. She was afraid she might be sick. They were going to search the house. And when they did, they would find the pint-size Ziploc bag containing almost an ounce of marijuana in the toe of her left black boot in her bedroom closet.

"Is your father home?" Officer Santino asked.

Courtney shook her head. "He's at the hospital."

"What is your name?" the woman asked.

"Courtney."

"Well, Courtney, I'm afraid we can't wait for your father to come home. But you can call him and tell him we're here, if that would make you more comfortable."

Courtney stared down at her socks, light gray with tiny navy blue flowers printed on them. "What are you doing here, anyway?"

"That's confidential," Officer Santino said. "But I can assure you it's police business."

Reluctantly, because she didn't seem to have a choice, Courtney stepped back and opened the door.

"Which room is Simon Gray's?" Sergeant Fowler asked.

The question caught Courtney by surprise. It hadn't once occurred to her that the police might be here because of Simon. They had come for *her,* hadn't they? "Upstairs, the second door on the right." She tried not to sound too relieved.

Sergeant Fowler headed up the stairs alone.

Courtney decided the woman was staying below to keep an eye on her. Maybe they considered her a suspect, too. "You said I could call my dad."

"Sure, go ahead." Lieutenant Santino smiled at Courtney, but Courtney didn't feel the least bit reassured. She headed straight for the phone in the kitchen and dialed a number, praying her father had his cell phone turned on. When she heard him bark "Hello" at the other end, she was actually relieved. Relief was not a feeling she associated with her father's voice.

"Dad, the police are here. They have a search warrant and want to see Simon's room."

"I'll be right home," he said.

Courtney still had the phone pressed to her ear when a loud humming sound signaled she had been disconnected.

Lieutenant Santino was peering out the front window in the living room, obviously interested in something outside. Courtney didn't stop to find out what; she headed right upstairs.

Sergeant Fowler was carefully removing the cables from Simon's computer. Courtney stood in the doorway of her brother's bedroom, watching him. The officer didn't glance up when she appeared, didn't say a word, as if walking off with someone's personal property was something he did every day. And maybe, Courtney thought, he did.

Simon's room was exactly as he had left it two days before. Nothing had changed, only the occupant was missing.

The room was almost Spartan. The bed was neatly made. No rugs on the floor, no curtains on the windows. The bookshelf was empty. Except for the computer, there was nothing on his desk. Unlike her own walls, papered to within an inch of their lives with posters of rock groups and rap stars, Simon's walls were bare.

Once, when she had asked him why his room was so empty, he had cocked his head to one side, looked at her in that puzzled way he had when he was trying to understand something, and said, "Why do people always feel they have to fill up every ounce of empty space with junk? I like my room this way. It's got all sorts of possibilities."

When Courtney told him she thought his room was totally impersonal, he'd laughed and said, "But it's *very* personal. It keeps them guessing." Courtney had had no idea what he was talking about, or what he meant by "them." But now, as she watched this stranger disconnecting the cables on Simon's PC, she thought how Simon hadn't left this man—or anyone else, for that matter—a single clue about who he was, what he liked, or what he thought. He even refused to wear anything with a designer's name on it. You couldn't pay him to wear brand-name clothes.

Sergeant Fowler lifted the computer from the top of Simon's desk, leaving behind the monitor, keyboard, and mouse, and headed back downstairs.

Lieutenant Santino was waiting by the front door. She opened it to let the sergeant through just as Simon's father came running across the lawn from the driveway. "What the hell do you think you're doing?" he shouted. The sergeant never missed a beat; he tipped his chin in the lieutenant's direction and kept on walking. Russell Gray stood with his mouth hanging open, watching him.

He turned to the lieutenant and Courtney, looked from one to the other, and apparently decided it was less of a risk to yell at his daughter. "Well, don't just stand there," he said, "call . . ." His voice trailed off.

"Dad," Courtney moaned, mortified to the brink of tears for both of them.

"I know, I know." His pale hand flopped back and forth. His sweaty face had turned a bright pink. He shook his head, looking embarrassed. "I haven't slept in almost two days," he told the lieutenant. "My son's in the hospital."

Lieutenant Santino nodded and said she knew about Simon, was sorry to hear about the accident. Courtney was surprised by the genuine look of sympathy on her face.

"I know this isn't a good time for us to be here, Mr. Gray," Lieutenant Santino said, "but we don't have a choice. I'll need you to come inside while I ask you a few questions."

"About what?" Russell Gray didn't budge an inch from his spot on the bottom step of the front porch. "What is this all about, anyway? What right have you to come barging into my house at a time like this?"

"Your son," Lieutenant Santino said, calmly, "could be in a great deal of trouble."

Courtney watched her father's face with interest. Surely the lieutenant was mistaken. Didn't she realize she was talking about Simon the Good? Saint Simon. The Simon who had never been in trouble. The Simon who was their father's pride and joy. The future CEO of a large software corporation. The son who was going to justify their father's existence and maybe make them all rich to boot. She was not at all surprised to see every last ounce of color drain right out of her father's face. With the dark smudges beneath his eyes and two days' worth of stubble on his pale face, he looked like a corpse. A sad, pathetic corpse. Courtney turned away. She couldn't bear to look at him.

That was when she noticed the black Mustang parked about halfway up the block on the other side of the street. It looked like Danny Giannetti's car, but it wasn't Danny in the front seat. A man, or maybe a boy, wearing dark sunglasses, sat behind the wheel. The back of his head was pressed against the headrest and his arms were folded as if he were napping. But Courtney wasn't so sure he was really asleep. His head was tilted in such a way that for all she knew he could be looking straight at them, watching their every move.

Later that afternoon, after school, Danny was mowing the lawn when Charlie Atwater pulled into the driveway in Danny's Mustang. The only thing Danny had to mow were wild shoots of onion grass. It was too early in the season to be mowing the lawn and he knew it. But it was something to do, something that allowed him to be outside, where he could keep an eye out for Charlie.

Charlie unfolded his long, gangly body from Danny's car and tossed a cigarette stub on the lawn. Ordinarily the thought of smoke stinking up the interior of his Mustang would have sent Danny into a rage, but he had bigger problems right now. He could tell by the look on Charlie's face that the news wasn't good.

"Not here," he said, before Charlie even opened his mouth.

Charlie shrugged and jammed his hands into the back pockets of his jeans. His short hair was bleached almost white and stood out at odd angles on top of his head. He was a classmate of Danny's, although he rarely bothered to show up for school. Most of the time he hung out down in Phillipsburg or across the river in Easton. Some of the kids thought he was into dealing drugs. But Danny figured if that were true, Charlie wouldn't waste his time doing surveillance work for the measly fifty dollars the three of them had scraped together. He would have brushed

Danny off like a mosquito. Instead, he seemed to jump at the idea when Danny approached him.

Danny knew it was a risk, getting Charlie to do their spying for them, but none of them could afford to skip classes or do anything that might cast suspicion on them. So they had hired Charlie, who insisted on using Danny's car since he didn't want to call attention to his own during "surveillance." They hadn't told Charlie the real reason they'd hired him, only that they were worried about Simon, worried that he might be in some sort of trouble.

The two of them got back into the Mustang, where Danny grilled Charlie for information, paid him the fifty bucks, dropped him off on Main Street, two blocks over from the park, and headed straight to Kyle's.

Danny knew Mrs. Byrnes would be at the courthouse. He only hoped Kyle was home. His head was so messed up from Charlie's account of the raid on Simon's PC that when Devin answered Kyle's door, Danny thought he'd come to the wrong house.

But then Kyle came up behind Devin, rested his hands on her shoulders, and the world shifted into balance again. Danny slipped past them both without an invitation.

"Is anybody else here?" he said. He flopped into his usual place, the recliner by the fireplace.

Kyle shook his head. "Just us." He and Devin sat on the couch. "So what did you find out?"

"Charlie said two people showed up at Simon's. A man and a woman. They left with Simon's PC."

Devin pressed her fingers to her lips. "Oh my god."

"Cops?" Kyle asked.

Danny shrugged. "Yeah, Charlie figured they were. They weren't in uniform."

"I can't believe they're on to us this soon," Devin said. "I mean, it was only last Thursday Kyle overheard the conversation between Schroder and McCabe. No one unusual has been at the school; we've been checking out the computer science lab." She looked over at Kyle. "I thought Mr. McCabe was going to handle this himself."

"That's what he wanted to do," Kyle said. "Schroder's the one who wanted to get the police involved. It looks like she got her way."

Danny was fighting hard to keep his thoughts straight. Images of him standing in a courtroom, of the look on his parents' faces, of being locked up in some six-by-eight cell with no windows, had him rattled and near panic. He couldn't get the grim pictures out of his head. None of this was supposed to be happening. He had just gotten accepted by Dartmouth. He had plans. He had potential. Damn it, he had a *future*. And spending it behind bars was not part of the plan.

Kyle was going on about how the school administrators might have brought some computer consultants in over the weekend, maybe even the local police, although he didn't think they had a computer crimes division. Danny was barely listening. He was imagining the police at his own front door, his father standing there in his black T-shirt and black pants—clothes he still wore at his print shop, even though he had long since converted his business from letterpress to laser printing—scratching his head. A dark figure growing even darker as he listened to what the police had to say.

"Simon wouldn't let anything happen," he told Kyle. "He's too smart. You said he'd cover his tracks, and I'm pretty sure he did."

"Maybe the police are smarter," Devin said. She had her hand on Kyle's wrist and her grip was growing tighter by the minute. "They have their own computer experts."

"On the state level," Kyle said, loosening her fingers. "And maybe in a few of the counties, but I doubt our local force has that kind of setup." He got to his feet and began to pace. Although every window in the house was open, he was sweating. His T-shirt clung to him like a damp dish towel. "If anyone comes around asking questions, none of us knows anything."

"What if they come to us with evidence?" Danny said.

"Deny it," Kyle told him. "Deny everything. You know nothing about anything. You have no idea who or why anyone would break into the school's computer system."

"But if they have evidence?" Danny insisted.

"It will point to Simon. And right now he's not talking."

Chapter 5

If Simon Gray had not been trapped inside the dark envelope that was his mind, he might have felt the cool hospital sheets beneath him, heard the wheezing of the respirator, seen the different colored lines on the cardiac monitor undulating across the screen, felt his father's callused hand on the side of his face, and smelled his familiar scent—the chemical odor that clung to his clothes from the pharmaceutical plant where he worked. If Simon had not been in a coma, he would have told his father that this was not how he'd expected things to turn out. Not even close.

He would tell him how the strangest things had been happening. How he could sit on the side of Stanley Isaacson's bed without the nurses shooing him back to his room. How he could wander the halls of the hospital unseen. And how, at this very moment, he was shocked right down to his bare toes to find himself at home, in his own bedroom.

He wasn't at all sure how he'd gotten there, but he now understood it wasn't necessary to physically leave the hospital to go from one place to another. Each time, there was only the whooshing sound, the icy damp gray, and a few moments of disorientation before he realized he was no longer in his body. He also knew he wasn't in control of his destinations. Or at least he didn't seem to be.

He touched his face, ran his fingers across his eyes, as he had done the few other times he had found himself outside his body, and discovered, as on those occasions, that he wasn't wearing his glasses. Simon found this astonishing. For the first time in years, he could see everything clearly without glasses. Every shadow, every line of every piece of furniture, and every object were as sharp and visible and even in some ways as wondrous as when he was four years old.

Moonlight streaked through his window, creating shadows. His own shadow, even though he was standing right in front of the window, was disturbingly absent. And so, he now saw, was his computer, although the keyboard and monitor still sat on his desk. A sense of dread crept along his spine; his chest felt tight. He couldn't understand why he should feel this way.

This was his room. Of that much he was certain. Bare walls, no rugs or curtains. Once, when his sister told him she thought his room was totally impersonal, that even prison inmates put things on their walls, he'd snapped back with what he thought was a pretty good putdown about people who needed to fill every ounce of empty space with meaningless junk. He was talking about Courtney, of course. But he doubted she realized that. If he were being truthful with her, which of course he wasn't, he would have said he had no idea what to put on his walls. No idea what kind of curtains or rugs he wanted. In all honesty, he had no idea who he even was. Weren't you supposed to have at least some idea before you stuck it all up there on your walls for the whole world to see?

He stared down at his desk and wondered if Courtney had moved the PC to her room. She was always after him about hogging it. They were supposed to share the computer. But it didn't make sense that she would leave behind the keyboard and monitor. Still, he couldn't imagine where else his PC would be, and he would have headed straight down to Courtney's room to find out if the computer was there, except he didn't seem to be able to leave his own room. He was tied to it by some invisible force, like a kite caught in a tree, and he was only now beginning to think he might be there for a reason.

Outside, it had begun to snow. Without warning, the wind grew fierce, smashing wet snowflakes against the windowpane, rattling the glass.

Faint sounds of R&B echoed from somewhere outside his door. It wasn't the sort of music Courtney listened to; it wasn't rap or heavy metal. Maybe his dad had the radio on.

Sometimes when there was only the hum of the refrigerator or an air conditioner, or the steady drumming of rain, Simon thought he heard a whole orchestra playing music he'd never heard before. Not inside his head, like some annoying, repetitive tune or jingle that got stuck in your brain, but soft, beautiful music gently surrounding him, kissing his ears. Whenever that happened, he would close his eyes and listen, trying to make distinctions between the different woodwinds, between the violins and violas, although he didn't know the first thing about music, had never played an instrument in his life, and was even told by his sixth-grade music teacher that he was tone-deaf.

Over the years he had devised a theory that the music was a distortion produced by the white noise, but most of the time he didn't try to explain it. He just listened.

He liked heavy metal and rap well enough, but as far as he was concerned, it was all background for the chaos in his head. If the music fit what was going on inside him, he listened. Otherwise he blocked it out. But the music that sometimes came to him unbidden, that was something else altogether. He wondered if it had to do with the hum of his own internal rhythms, the music his body made, music no one but Simon could hear.

This was the first time he'd traveled beyond the hospital. Yet the chill of the hospital room and the smell of bleach were still with him. He was here and not here. There and not there. He had no idea how much time had passed—days, weeks, maybe even years. He wasn't sure what time of year it was. The sight of the snow muddled his brain. He sat on the edge of his bed and watched large feathery flakes land on tree branches thick with sleeping black crows, turning their feathers white.

Simon lay down. His hands cradled the back of his head. He stared up at the ceiling. The moonlight had disappeared behind clouds of snow. The shadows in the room had dissolved. But Simon's eyes were accustomed to the dark. He spent almost all his time there, except when he was dreaming or traveling outside his body.

He stared over at his desk and was suddenly reminded of Kyle. He saw the two of them in the library, Simon sitting in front of one of a half dozen computers, Kyle pointing to something on the screen, occasionally glancing over his shoulder to make sure no one else was watching them. Simon wished he hadn't thought of Kyle because now fragments of memories were seeping back into his mind. Outside, one of the crows lifted off a snowy branch, fluttered a black wing against the window, creating a lake of clear glass in the middle of the wet snow, and disappeared into the night.

He thought of Devin McCafferty, of the soft shell-pink lining of her delicate ears. Simon's heart began to pound. He saw her standing at the kitchen counter in Kyle's house last summer, sliding vegetables onto long metal skewers so Kyle's mother could grill them. When he came into the room, Devin spun around, grabbed an empty skewer, angled her arms and legs like a fencer, and thrust it toward him. *"En garde,"* she said, feigning a French accent. The skewer stopped within an inch of his heart. So close. Then she straightened up, holding the skewer end to end over her head with both hands, and grinned.

The image almost brought him to tears. He wanted her that badly. He had since the very first time he saw her on the playground of Bellehaven Elementary leaping into the air and catching Frisbees with the ease and grace of a gazelle because she was almost a full head taller than anyone else in the fourth grade. She was only a year ahead of him, but it might as well have been a century.

The night of Rob Fisher's party, Simon had thought he'd died and gone to heaven when Devin McCafferty came up to him in a ribbed tank top almost the color of her hair and told him she thought he looked like a younger version of Chad Lowe, except with curly hair, could maybe even pass for his son. Simon laughed because he didn't know what else to do; he wasn't even sure who Chad Lowe was, but he could tell by the look on Devin's face she meant it to be a compliment. Then she had taken him completely by surprise. She asked him if he wanted to dance, gently taking his hand before he could answer one way or the other and leading him to where others were dancing.

Simon knew Devin and Kyle had been together since their freshman year. Everyone in the school knew that. He knew he didn't stand a chance with her, knew she was probably asking him to dance because Kyle had told her to, knew he should have felt humiliated, outraged at Kyle. Instead, he found himself overwhelmed with gratitude. Glad for any crumbs Devin and Kyle wanted to toss his way. Until that moment he had believed that no matter how bad things got at school—the body slamming, the food dumped on his head at lunch, the jocks tripping him in the halls between classes—he always had his dignity, his self-respect. He was, and always would be, his own person.

Until Devin McCafferty laid her milk-white hand on his arm.

By the end of that night he had agreed to help Kyle and the others with their "project," the project they had begun in their sophomore year with Walter Tate as their stooge, their computer geek. Had Devin put her hand on Walter's arm, too? Asked him to dance? And even if she had, would it have made any difference?

After the night of the party, Simon became Walter's replacement. It had nothing to do with Kyle's smooth voice, assuring him that none of them were doing anything anyone else wasn't doing, although the means might be different. Nor did it have anything to do with Kyle's insistence that nobody got ahead in life without cheating at least some of the time, or with his rationale for how—things being so competitive these days and knowing that your competition was probably cheating—you had to do it just to keep up.

Simon had heard it all before. He hadn't bought it when other kids used these arguments as justification for cheating and he wasn't about to buy it now. Besides, he was only half listening. How could he concentrate with Devin sitting on the arm of his redwood chair, across from

Kyle on the Fishers' deck, the toes of one delicate bare foot pressed against the wood boards for support, the other foot, still in its open-backed sandal, swinging back and forth, her bare arm brushing against his own?

The music from down the hall had stopped. There were only the sounds of the wind and the brittle branches beating on the window of his room. Simon wondered what he would do if he could go back in time, change everything that had happened that year. And without a moment's hesitation he knew he would do it all over again. He would do it for the same reason, the only reason, he'd done it the first time—for Devin.

The freak snowstorm barreled through at a ferocious speed, knocking the wind right out of everything in its path—people, animals, and budding plants. Winter had returned for one last stand. One day the temperature reaches eighty-nine degrees and you're baking on the lounge chair in your backyard, oiled all over with Coppertone. The next day you're slathering Vaseline Intensive Care all over your face to protect it from the stinging sleet and wind while you scrape off the windshield of your car. One minute you're digging out tank tops from the bottom dresser drawer where you stashed them last September and packing away wool sweaters, and the next thing you know icicles are dangling from the eaves of the roof. While the magnolia's fragile buds shiver in the bitter wind, daffodils are dashed to the ground beneath heavy wet snow. Already the flowers on the plum trees are turning brown. And mushy flowers from the forsythia ooze like butter between your thumb and forefinger.

The residents of Bellehaven stood on their front stoops, snow shovels in hand, or in front of their garages, filling their snowblowers with gasoline, and shook their heads. They stared out at the scene, numbed by Nature's savage betrayal.

Liz Shapiro could have cared less. She welcomed the weight of wet snow on her shovel as she slowly made her way down the front walk. Each heavy load stretched her muscles to the limit, straining her chest, pulling at her heart, making the other ache, the one deep inside, seem momentarily bearable.

The sharp glare of sun on snow helped to blur images of Simon hooked up to a tangle of tubes that would keep him alive until he was ready to come back to her. Courtney hadn't spared a single detail when she described his condition to her two days before. And now Liz couldn't get these disturbing pictures out of her mind. She hoped Simon, in his coma, couldn't feel pain.

She looked over at the magnolia. Only an hour earlier her mother, bundled into her plaid flannel robe, had stood by the window with a mug of coffee in her hand, while tears of disappointment streamed down her cheeks at the sight of the snow-covered tree. She had waited weeks for the blossoms to open. Now that wasn't going to happen. The next day or the day after that, the buds would turn brown, then crispy, like so many ugly cocoons. Nothing would burst forth from them. No lovely pink-white blossoms. Not now. Liz had seen this happen before, buds tricked by days of warm sunlight into almost blooming, only to be stunned, stunted, destroyed by a heavy biting spring frost. A horrible, cruel joke.

Liz had finished the front walk and was working on the sidewalk when she spotted Devin McCafferty heading toward her, her jacket unzipped and billowing in the wind, her head hatless, her red hair blowing every which way as she tried to keep her balance on platform boots that weren't made for snow.

Devin stopped a few feet away and patiently waited for Liz to shovel the last few feet of the sidewalk.

Liz couldn't imagine what Devin was doing here. It wasn't like they hung out together, although sometimes Liz tagged along with Simon when he went to a game with Kyle and his friends. Once she had even gone with them to a party, but she'd left early because she'd felt disconcertingly invisible.

She didn't even like Devin, particularly. She had seen the way Simon looked at her whenever they were all together. It killed her to admit it, but Simon was in love with Devin. And there wasn't a thing she could do about it.

"We went to see him," Devin told her when Liz finally stopped shoveling. "Last night."

Liz knew she was talking about Simon. "In this blizzard?"

"It wasn't snowing when we left for the hospital."

"Who's 'we'?"

"Kyle and I, of course."

"How did you get into the ICU? I thought only immediate family could visit patients in there."

Devin breathed an impatient sigh. "We sneaked in."

"Why?" Liz leaned her weight on the snow shovel as if she expected it to hold her up. She was so jealous she felt physically sick.

"Well, to see how he's doing. Why else?" Devin looked away. She pretended to be watching the windows of Liz's house. "We only had a few minutes with him before we got caught."

Liz wished she had tried to sneak in to see Simon last Monday, instead of letting his father send her home.

"He looked bad. I mean, *really* bad." Devin kicked at a small unshoveled clump of snow with the toe of her boot. "They shaved part of his head, and he's got these bandages . . . and there are all these tubes and machines . . ." Her voice trailed off.

Liz felt something icy in the pit of her stomach. It was obvious Devin was expecting the worst. Liz could see it in her face. Devin didn't think Simon was going to make it.

Being superstitious, Liz wanted to grab Devin and shake her, tell her even thinking such a horrible thing might be bad luck. Instead, she stared down at her boots, uncertain what to do next. She had finished shoveling the walk and wanted to go back in the house, crash on the couch with a bag of potato chips, and watch the soaps all afternoon, although she knew she should spend the day working on her history paper for Mrs. Rosen. The deadline was a week from Friday.

She couldn't figure out what Devin was doing there and was beginning to wonder if maybe she had something more to say, since it didn't look as if she was in any hurry to leave.

From overhead the crows, balanced on snowy branches, cocked their heads as if straining to hear what the girls would say next. One of them broke ranks and swooped toward a snowbank by the street, picked up a soggy red twist-tie in its beak, then lifted back into the air when it suddenly spotted Devin's red hair blowing in all directions. Before either girl saw it coming, the bird dropped the twist-tie and dove straight for Devin's hair, sending her into fits of hysteria.

She plunged her black leather boots into the snowy front yard, flailing her arms over her head and shrieking. Liz, a few feet behind her, swatted at the bird with the snow shovel, missing it only by inches, until the crow finally gave up, retrieved the twist-tie, and headed for the nearest tree.

"God, it's like being in that old Hitchcock movie. They're getting worse every day." Devin headed up the front steps and grabbed the door handle, even though she hadn't been invited in. "And nobody's doing anything about them. Like, you'd think they were an endangered species or something, instead of maniacs with feathers and a license to attack on sight."

Liz didn't say a word. She let Devin walk right into her house because she couldn't think of any reason not to.

Once inside, Devin blinked and looked around awkwardly, as if she had just realized she'd barged right into someone's home without being asked. "I wanted to get away from that kamikaze bird, is all." She gave Liz an embarrassed, apologetic look. "I'll leave in a minute."

Mrs. Shapiro was standing at the end of the hall in the doorway leading to the kitchen. She was still wearing her flannel robe. Strands of her dark shoulder-length hair had escaped the claw clip. She glanced up from the pages of a manuscript she held in her hand and sized up Devin.

Liz was embarrassed, as much for her mother as for herself, although she was used to her mother working in her bathrobe, sometimes until late afternoon if she was in the middle of a book. "This is Devin," she said awkwardly. "From school."

Mrs. Shapiro smiled at Devin, nodded, then shifted her gaze to Liz. "You're going to shovel the back walk, too, right? I wouldn't ask if your dad wasn't in Zürich." Mr. Shapiro, a chemist at the pharmaceutical plant on the outskirts of town, had left for a conference in Switzerland the weekend before.

Devin said, "Guess I'd better go." She clamped her hand around the front doorknob but didn't make any effort to turn it. Without looking at Liz, she mumbled to the door, "You want to go to the mall or something?"

Liz wasn't sure she'd heard her right. Was Devin McCafferty asking if she wanted to hang out at the mall with her? With more than a half foot of snow outside, trees black with crows, and now this latest paradox, Liz was beginning to think she might have awakened in a parallel universe that morning.

"Well?" Devin turned the knob and opened the door.

Liz knew if she stayed home her mother would probably find all sorts of chores for her to do. If not, she still had to face that history paper on Jessup Wildemere. "I'll shovel the other walk when I get back from the mall," she called over her shoulder and headed out the door before her mother could object.

As soon as they were outside, Devin said, "So can you get your mom's car?"

"You're kidding. You heard her. I'm supposed to be shoveling the back walk. Can't you get a car?"

Devin shook her head. "My mom went in to work today. I'm supposed to be watching the other kids." When Liz stared back at her, Devin shrugged. "I got tired of wiping jelly fingerprints off the TV screen."

"So, what? They're home alone?"

"My sister Katy's watching them. She's almost fifteen. She can handle it." Devin stood at the end of the front walk, shivering, her bare hands stuffed in her jacket pockets.

Liz looked up at Devin's face. She shaded her eyes with her hand to keep the glare of the sun on the snow from blinding her. She knew Devin had other friends she could go to the mall with. Friends with cars. She wondered if maybe Devin needed to talk to someone about Simon, someone who knew him better than anyone.

A car zipped by, spraying slush from the road onto the sidewalk; wet chunks of dirty snow clung to the bottoms of their jeans. But neither girl seemed to notice. Devin looked up and down the street before she said, her voice low, "I guess we take the bus, then."

Danny chugged the last of his birch beer and pushed his half-eaten hot dog and fries to the side. He and Kyle had spent the morning in Mr. Giannetti's Jeep plowing driveways for extra cash. Danny had bought the secondhand plow himself the year before, and it had more than paid for itself. When it looked as if they weren't going to drum up any more business, they stopped at Hot Dog Dottie's out on Route 40 to get something to eat.

Danny had spent most of the morning obsessing over what they'd do if the police found something on Simon's computer. "You're getting your shorts in a knot over nothing," Kyle told him. "Simon's too smart to leave any evidence lying around. And if they do find something, it's Simon who's going down."

"Unless he talks."

"How's he going to do that?" Kyle, who had polished off all his French fries, took a couple from Danny's plate. "He's in a coma. Nobody's going to try and prosecute some kid at death's door." He grinned, biting into the fries. "It'd look bad, especially in an election year. Public sympathy counts in the polls. Look at my uncle Jim; he's on the town council. He doesn't make a move unless the mayor gives him a green light. And the mayor doesn't do anything that's not going to get him reelected."

Danny sighed and looked away. He stared out the front window of Dottie's place at the steep mounds of snow framing the parking lot. Crows were waddling back and forth along the tops, keeping a precarious balance.

When he was maybe four or five years old, he used to pretend the mounds left by the plows were snow-covered mountains to be conquered. He'd dig little footholds, making his way carefully to the top.

"He could come out of the coma any day, any minute, for that matter," Danny said.

Earlier that morning, as they plowed the Lehmans' driveway, Kyle had told Danny about how he and Devin had sneaked into Simon's room the night before. Now he looked over at Danny and shook his head. "You wouldn't think so if you'd seen him last night."

Danny considered this. Was Kyle saying that Simon wasn't going to recover? It wasn't that this thought hadn't occurred to him before. He just preferred not to think about it. "You know, even if Simon does come out of the coma and the cops grill him, I don't think he'll talk," he told Kyle. Danny desperately needed to convince himself that this was true. Simon considered them his friends. He was the kind of guy who would take the blame for all of them if it came down to it.

"You about done with that thing?" Kyle said. He pointed to Danny's hot dog. "I've got to get home and study for a math test tomorrow."

Danny picked up the half-eaten hot dog, decided he wasn't hungry, and dropped it back on the plate. "Study?"

"We're on our own right now, remember?" Kyle stood and pulled the hood of his sweatshirt over his head. "If my grades slip, I can forget Harvard."

Danny nodded and followed Kyle out the door, although he didn't see what Kyle was worried about. Even with "the project," Kyle studied hard; he had top scores on his SATs. He would probably have gotten into Harvard without Simon's help. He just wasn't taking any chances. Danny was beginning to feel a little queasy about this college business himself. If he didn't keep his grades up through the rest of the year, there was a good chance the admissions directors at Dartmouth would change their minds.

Recently, he had begun to wonder what he would do when he got to Dartmouth. Because once he was there, once classes started in the fall, there wouldn't be any Simon Gray to steal passwords to help him get into the system, to help him get copies of exams in advance.

If he thought about this for too long he would begin to panic. Instead, he told himself there would be other Simons, probably a whole bunch of computer geeks just ripe for the picking. If you pushed all the right buttons—and he'd watched Kyle do that for three years now, first with Walter, then Simon—you could get them to show off what they could do.

One of the crows lifted off a mound of snow and landed on the hood of Danny's Jeep. It paraded back and forth in front of the windshield. He leaned out the window and shouted, "Stupid-ass bird. You scratch the paint on my dad's Jeep and you're history." When the bird continued to pace, Danny jumped out of the Jeep and swatted it so hard it landed in a snowbank, stunned but still breathing.

He turned to look at Kyle, who was staring through the

windshield at the crow. "We can't leave everything to chance," Kyle told him.

"Meaning?"

"Meaning if Simon comes out of that coma, we can't just assume he won't talk. We should have a plan, in case things don't go our way."

Danny turned the key in the ignition but made no attempt to back out of the parking space. "What kind of plan?" Judging by the expression on Kyle's face, he wasn't at all sure he wanted an answer to this question. But Kyle only shrugged and turned his face away to look out the side window. All he said was "I'll have to get back to you on that."

Chapter 6

Devin held up a lime green sweater for Liz's consideration. After walking the mile to Route 40 and catching the bus to the mall, they were rummaging through one of the sales tables at the Gap. Devin couldn't for the life of her figure out why she'd asked Liz to go to the mall. It wasn't like they were friends or anything. Vaguely, she wondered if it had something to do with Simon, then pushed the thought to the back of her mind.

"The color's not bad," Liz told her. "For you, anyway."

Devin didn't miss Liz's indifference. What was she doing asking Liz Shapiro, of all people, for her opinion on clothes? The girl hardly ever wore anything that wasn't black, except for blue jeans once in a while. Devin doubted Liz had any color sense at all. And it was obvious shopping was the last thing on Liz's mind. Devin felt the same way. She was just killing time until . . . what? Until the police found hard evidence on Simon's computer or one of the computers at school? Until she and the others were caught and forced into a confession? Until one of them cracked and they all turned themselves in? She tried not to laugh at this last image. It was so B-movie melodramatic.

All the bright summer colors—bold violet, tangerine, daffodil yellow—under the glare of the fluorescent lights were making her dizzy. Her eyes hurt. One side of her head had begun to throb. She thought she might be getting a migraine.

"I'm going to try it on," Devin said and headed for the dressing room. She didn't even like the sweater and knew she wasn't going to buy it. But for some reason she needed to get away from the harsh lights and all those customers who were digging through the neatly stacked piles of new tank tops and tees. She needed someplace to be alone, someplace to think.

Inside the dressing room she tossed the sweater on the bench and stared down at it. Her heart was pounding so hard she could barely take a breath, as if she'd been running nonstop for miles. She caught a glimpse of her reflection in the mirror, eyes wide, her skin so pale and taut with tension that fine blue veins had appeared above her brow. Her mass of red hair was still tangled from the icy wind outside. She didn't know this girl at all, this stranger, this crazy person, staring back at her.

Until the day before, she had been able to hold on to

some thin thread of hope, the belief that somehow they would all get through this unscathed, that Kyle would never let them get caught and Simon would never be so stupid as to leave evidence behind, especially on his computer. People committed crimes all the time and never got caught. Why should she and the others be any different?

Suddenly she found herself wishing Simon were there. She missed him and that surprised her. If he'd been there, he would have put his arm around her shoulders and reassured her with that funny half-cocked smile of his. He would have given the ends of her hair a light tug. He'd have said, "McCafferty, you're getting all uptight over nothing."

Am I? she wondered.

Devin took several deep breaths and tried to calm down. The night before at the hospital, when she and Kyle had sneaked into Simon's room, it had been all she could do not to scream out loud when she saw him lying there, so exposed and vulnerable.

She and Kyle had waited for almost a half hour to find an unobtrusive way to enter the intensive care unit. They had discovered that the only way in was to press a large circular plate outside the heavy metal double doors leading into the unit. A large sign was posted on one of the doors: *Immediate Family Only.* After they'd watched one of the doctors press the plate and heard the clatter of the doors opening, they knew the noise would draw attention to anyone who tried to enter.

Finally, they had followed a man and woman into the ICU who were obviously there to visit someone. As soon as the doors thumped open, Devin and Kyle did a quick survey of the large room, a surprisingly cheerful place with pale mauve walls and a flowered border that ran along the top, right below the ceiling. On the left were rooms, only one of which had the curtain drawn across the glass wall. The others appeared to be unoccupied.

The first station, presumably for the administrative assistants, was empty. The second, farther back in the room, appeared to be the nurses' station. Only two nurses were on duty, and they were busy talking with the man and woman who had just entered the room.

Kyle nudged Devin and tipped his head toward the second room on the left, the one with the partially pulled curtain. He slid the glass door to the side and the two of them slipped into the room.

Devin was glad Simon's room wasn't on the other side of the nurses' station. They would have never been able to pull this off.

With the curtain closed over the single window and the curtain pulled across most of the glass wall, dimming the glare of the fluorescent lights from the main room, Devin could barely make out the form on the bed. Simon's face was bruised and swollen. He looked so different that at first Devin thought they had the wrong room. The person lying in the bed barely resembled the boy who had become such an indispensable cog in their crooked wheel. She grabbed the cold metal side rail and held on so tightly both hands turned waxy white.

If the nurse hadn't shown up at that moment and ushered them back through the double doors, Devin might have bolted right out of the room on her own. The sight of Simon was far worse than she had imagined.

But there had been a single moment, while Kyle attempted to charm the nurse into letting them stay, when Devin had managed to unglue her hand from the metal bar and rest it on Simon's. "Simon," she whispered. "I miss you." And then she and Kyle were brusquely escorted back to the waiting room.

Kyle stood in the middle of the cramped room, his hands in the pockets of his cargo pants, staring at the hospital's mission statement posted on the wall, looking thoughtful. Devin, not realizing he wasn't behind her, was already halfway down the hall, heading for the front lobby before she noticed. And she would have kept on going, Kyle or no Kyle, if she hadn't made a wrong turn, ending up in another ward. As she stood in the hall, trying to get her bearings, images of Simon lying in that hospital bed came crashing down on her. He was going to die. Anyone could see that. No one who looked that bad could be expected to survive.

This was all their fault, hers and Kyle's and Danny's. They should never have dragged him into "the project." He didn't have Walter Tate's devious nature.

Another, more disturbing thought came to her. What if Simon had been so upset about the possibility of an investigation, terrified of what would happen to his reputation, that he had run into the Hanging Tree on purpose? That was when Devin began to sob uncontrollably. She could not stop shaking. Simon was going to die and there was nothing she could do about it.

Kyle rounded the corner just as a concerned nurse came running from behind her station. Kyle put his arm around Devin and steered her away from the oncoming woman.

"Jeez, Dev. What the hell is wrong with you?" he said, keeping his voice low.

"Simon," she told him between sobs. "He's going to die, isn't he?"

"He's not going to die, okay? Get a grip, for god's sake."

As soon as they reached the lobby Kyle said, "Nothing like making a scene so they'll be sure to remember us here."

"What's that supposed to mean?"

He fumbled in his pocket for his car keys as they stepped through the automatic sliding doors leading outside. "It's not what I'd call keeping a low profile."

Devin was too exhausted and shaken from seeing Simon to argue with Kyle. Still, she wondered, as she often found herself doing these days, what she had ever seen in Kyle. Sometimes she marveled that they had been together for almost four years.

Someone was tapping lightly on the louvered door to the dressing room. Liz's voice floated into the cramped space.

"Devin? Are you okay?"

"Fine."

"You've been in there twenty minutes. How long does it take to try on one sweater?"

Devin drew a long breath. "I can't decide whether to buy it or not."

"So put it back on the table. We can come back later if you still want it."

Before she realized what was happening, Devin was sliding down the wall of the dressing room. She landed on her backside, knees up against her chest. She couldn't seem to get up.

"Can I come in?" Liz asked. Her voice sounded cautious. It was obvious she knew something was wrong. When Devin didn't respond, Liz tried the doorknob but found the door locked. Below was an open space of about one foot. She peeked under the door, then got down on her hands and knees and scooted underneath. She leaned against the wall across from Devin, her back against the mirror. "So, what? Do you want to go home?"

Home. Devin closed her eyes. All these years she had been looking forward to the moment when she could leave the crowded Cape Cod house on Meadowlark Drive, when she would share a room with only one other person, not two, when she wouldn't have to elbow out eight other people plus her grandparents for a fried chicken breast. And now it seemed that in ways she had never expected, she had already left. The Devin who walked through the back door that night would not be the same girl who'd left the house late that morning, would never be the same girl. It was almost, she thought, as if everything that had come before had suddenly been canceled out. This was what was left, this panicked pale face in the mirror, a face she couldn't even bring herself to look at.

Liz leaned forward. Gently she placed a warm reassuring hand on Devin's. "Come on. We'll leave, okay? The bus should be outside in about ten minutes."

But Devin had begun to cry. Tears snaked streaks of mascara down her cheeks. And there was nothing Liz could do but wait.

Liz sat cross-legged on her unmade bed surrounded by note cards and library books. Her smoky-gray cat, Pandora, was curled in her lap, warming herself in the late-afternoon sun that spread over Liz's legs and the bunched-up comforter. Liz stroked the cat. She bent over and rubbed the tip of her nose in Pandora's fur. The last thing she felt like doing was working on her history paper. Whatever had possessed her to write about Jessup Wildemere, for Pete's sake? Whatever made her think she could find some undiscovered bit of information from some remote event that had happened more than two hundred years earlier? All she had to go on were the same stories her parents and grandparents and those before them had grown up with—stories told around campfires late at night, or at Halloween parties where the only light came from candles burning inside hollow pumpkins.

Everyone in Bellehaven knew how Jessup Wildemere, a scraggly, unsavory drifter, had stabbed Cornelius Dobbler so many times the blood had seeped through the crevices in the floorboards and stained the ceiling below, and how he'd been caught the very same night by some of the townsmen.

The hanging had taken place during the snow-blistering

winter of 1798, back when the town was still called Havenhill, back when food was scarce and the townsfolk couldn't see sharing what little they had with some murderer locked up in the jail for what could be months before a judge ever came through and tried the case, if at all. So they took matters into their own hands, had a brisk, tidy trial in the local tavern with a preacher presiding over the proceedings, found Jessup Wildemere guilty as sin, and hanged him the next morning before the sun was up and before they'd have to feed him breakfast.

Jessup Wildemere was the only person ever to be executed in the entire county. And it wasn't even legal.

Campfire ghost stories aside, Liz had begun to wonder if she would ever find any records of the case. No one seemed to know why Jessup had killed Cornelius Dobbler, although there was much speculation. Some claimed he had been drunk, others said it had to do with an argument, still others suggested he was flat-out insane. Pure and simple.

Liz had spent hours in the archives of the library and at the local historical society. So far she had turned up very little. Not only was the lack of historical evidence discouraging, but she had more or less lost her enthusiasm for the project when she'd learned of Simon's accident. She could no longer think of the Hanging Tree—as everyone at school called it—without thinking of Simon.

The whole project, just the thought of anything to do with the Hanging Tree, seemed even more impossible since Devin had told her earlier that day how bad Simon had looked in the hospital. Devin's words had been nowhere near as revealing as the expression on her face, a look that clearly said she feared for Simon's life.

Liz squeezed her eyes closed and tried to picture Simon as he was the summer when they were both thirteen and racing each other to the floating dock in the middle of Silver Lake—the summer she fell in love with him. She had been pulling ahead of him, digging hard at the water, determined to beat him, when she felt a hand on her ankle. It was Simon. With one swift yank, he dove beneath the water and pulled her with him. Liz had grabbed his hair, kicked her feet, and flailed her arms, trying to get to the surface.

Both of them had shot through the water at the same time. Waterfalls streamed from Simon's joyous face as his mouth burst open in surprise laughter. His arms circled her waist as he lifted her into the air. And when he lowered her into the water, their faces were barely a breath apart. She would have kissed him right then and there, if he hadn't suddenly pushed off in the direction of the dock, never once looking back. If he had, he would have realized that Liz, who remained exactly where he'd left her, stunned and treading water, had forgotten all about the race.

Carefully, Liz slid Pandora from her lap and went to the window, using her foot to plow a path between clothes, books, and food-crusted plates along the way. The sun had dipped behind the house across the street, leaving soft purple shadows on the snow. If she opened the window and leaned out far enough, she could catch a glimpse of a few of the top branches of the Hanging Tree, a block and a half away. Even though the tree was on the same road as the high school, Liz had managed to avoid it by crossing to the other side of the street, going around the block to Greenwood Avenue, and then heading down to Edgewood. Now she wondered how she was ever going to write a paper on Jessup Wildemere if she couldn't even bring herself to walk by the tree where he was hanged.

Liz glanced over at Pandora, who slid to the edge of the bed on her belly, slowly stretched out both front legs, and dropped gracefully to the floor. The cat sidled up to her and threaded herself in and around Liz's legs.

"You're right," she said to the cat, as if Pandora had spoken. "I can't spend the rest of my life avoiding that stupid tree." She reached over, snapped up her jacket from the back of her desk chair, and headed downstairs.

Fortunately, despite the mounds of snow hiding the curb, the sidewalks were clear. It hadn't occurred to her to put on boots.

As she neared the end of Willowbrook Road, her heart began to thump uncontrollably. On the corner was the Gulf station and across the street from it, the Liberty Tree. The icy wind whipped the branches of the old oak into a frenzy and brought tears to Liz's eyes. She pulled the hood of her jacket over her head.

For a while, she stood on the corner and stared over at the tree. She wondered how it was going to survive with such a huge gash cut into it, a gash made by Simon's Honda. The wound had been covered with pitch. But Liz had her doubts.

She stuffed her hands in her coat pockets and crossed the street, coming to stand only a few feet from the snow piled by the curb. The bronze plaque, she saw, lay bent and semiburied in the snow. Maybe a snowplow had hit it, but she doubted it. The people who drove the plows knew to keep their distance from the tree. More than likely it was Simon's car that had damaged the plaque.

Liz shifted her gaze from the plaque to the branches above her head, branches, like most trees in Bellehaven these days, laden with crows. She wondered which branch had supported Jessup Wildemere's body. But most of all, she wondered how she was ever going to get to the truth of what had happened in this place. Both times.

Simon was walking down the hospital corridor next to Courtney. He could hardly believe it. A few minutes before—or maybe hours or days, he could never be sure—he'd thought he heard her voice. It had floated down to him, echoed off stone walls, as if he lay at the bottom of a well. He tried to answer, as he lay there in the cold dark, tried to see some light, some indication of how far down in the well he might be, tried to gauge how long it might take before someone found him.

And now here he was, walking beside his sister, wondering how she'd managed to pull him out of the well and whether she'd come to take him home. Except, like everyone else in the hospital, she didn't seem aware he was there. Simon opened his mouth to ask her what had happened to him, to ask why he was in this place, but no words came out.

Before he could decide what to do to get her attention, he felt the clammy gray chill. Fully expecting to be pulled back into his body, he wasn't prepared to find himself outside, standing beneath the Liberty Tree. Worse yet, he was still in his flimsy hospital gown. Instinctively he reached behind him to make sure the ties were knotted securely. The snow covered his ankles, yet he felt no icy sting on his legs or bare feet.

The base of the bronze plaque had been bent all the way to the ground, and the plaque itself was half hidden beneath the snow, as if someone had plowed right into it. The sun had already dropped behind the trees, but Simon could still make out a gash the size of a huge beach ball. The wound had jagged edges, as if a *T. rex* had taken a bite out of the lower part of the ancient oak. Someone had painted thick globs of tar over it.

Chills rippled along his spine. The sight of the gash disturbed him, although he didn't know why. Nor did he know why he had come to this place. One minute he'd thought he was on his way home with Courtney, and the next . . .

For the first time since he'd appeared in this place, Simon noticed a young man, his body hunched forward, sitting on the Neidermeyers' split-rail fence on the other side of the sidewalk. The man studied him with curiosity. Behind him, the evening sky had begun to turn a midnight blue. Simon realized the man actually *saw* him. The only other person to see him had been Stanley Isaacson. Simon grabbed the back of his gown, held it tightly closed. But if the man noticed anything odd about the way Simon was dressed, he didn't let on.

Simon, however, was acutely aware of the man's clothes. They were like nothing he'd ever seen, except perhaps in history books—black breeches, knitted stockings, worn dusty black shoes with large buckles, an off-white shirt, and a tan vest. On this unusually bitter cold day the man wasn't even wearing a coat. His long dark hair was pulled back and tied at the base of his neck with a black ribbon. On his head he wore a tricornered hat.

The man nodded but said nothing. He slid from the split-rail fence, landed solidly on his feet, and strutted over to the base of the tree. He walked with an easy gait, as if there weren't a half foot of snow on the ground, and leaned one shoulder against the bark. If he saw the tar-patched gash, he didn't mention it. Folding his arms, he looked straight at Simon.

Just then, Mr. Neidermeyer came out of his front door and began to sweep snow from the steps of his porch. A plaid wool scarf, wrapped about the lower part of his face, covered his gray beard. His wool cap was pulled down so far, all Simon could make out was the glare from the porch light glinting off the lenses of the old man's glasses.

Simon waved and shouted hello. This was a test. He wanted to see if the rules here by the Liberty Tree were the same as in the hospital. And apparently they were because just like the doctors and nurses, Mr. Neidermeyer never looked up, didn't even hear him.

But when Simon turned back to the stranger, the man

stared at him as if he'd completely lost his mind. "Who are you shouting to?"

Simon looked back at the Neidermeyer house to confirm what he saw. Certain he was seeing what he thought he was, he said, "Mr. Neidermeyer."

The man shook his head, obviously bewildered. "I see no one in that pasture."

What was he talking about? Pasture? There was no pasture. There was only the Neidermeyer house and front yard. Simon tried to wrap his mind around the inconceivable. He was beginning to realize this man couldn't see the Neidermeyers' house, couldn't see Mr. Neidermeyer sweeping the snow from his steps. He had no idea how that could be. "You don't see a house there?" Simon asked him.

A brash wind shook the branches overhead, thrust clumps of snow to the ground. Simon jumped back to avoid getting clobbered, but the man didn't seem to notice the snow or the wind. Loose strands of his hair, Simon saw, didn't even move. But then, neither did Simon's own hair or his hospital gown. Yet all around them branches rattled like brittle bones.

"A house?" The man turned to look again, then shook his head.

"You were sitting on the Neidermeyers' fence," Simon said, pointing to the split rails.

"You mean Joseph Alderman's fence. And a fine job we did on it, too. I spent most of the summer helping him." The man pulled at his chin, looking thoughtful. "Though this drought makes for poor grazing. Joseph will likely lose some of his cows before winter."

Simon stared down at the snow and back at the man. "You don't see the snow, either, do you?"

The man let out a surprised laugh. "Snow? This time of year?"

Simon's heart had begun to beat faster. "What time of year is it?"

"Don't you know your seasons, lad?" The man spread his arms skyward. "It's late summer, of course." He narrowed his eyes suspiciously. "Where do you hail from, friend?"

"From right here," Simon said. "Bellehaven."

"Bellehaven? Surely you are mistaken. This is the village of Havenhill. And I, young sir, am Jessup Wildemere, at your service." The man swept his hat from his head, clicked his heels together, and made a polite bow. "And you would be . . . ?"

Simon told the man his name, all the while thinking someone was playing an elaborate joke on him. This man couldn't possibly be Jessup Wildemere, not the same drifter who was hanged from the branches of the Liberty Tree—the Hanging Tree, the very tree they both now stood beneath—for murdering Cornelius Dobbler. Simon stared at the man in disbelief. Like every kid in school, he knew the story of Jessup Wildemere.

Simon had always imagined Jessup Wildemere in smelly, sweat-stained buckskins, with a grizzly lice-laden beard and brown rotting teeth. But the man who stood before him was young, only a few years older than he, and well dressed. Or at least as far as Simon could tell. He looked like a decent enough person. Not at all like someone who could commit murder.

"What are you doing here?" Simon all but whispered the question. He felt foolish even asking it. Because by now it seemed obvious to him that this was a dream. It had to be. Jessup Wildemere had been dead more than two hundred years. Things like this didn't happen when you were awake.

The man looked beyond Simon and smiled. "I'm waiting for someone."

Simon knew that smile, had felt it on his own face many times. It was the same look he got whenever Devin McCafferty walked into view.

But just as his lips parted, about to form the question "Who?" Simon felt the pull of his body and the painful plunge back into dark silence.

Chapter 7

BY NOON ON FRIDAY ALL THE SNOW EXCEPT THE mounds left by the plows had melted. The magnolia buds had already begun to turn brown. A warm spring breeze carried an invisible airborne cloud from the pharmaceutical plant into town. It hovered over the houses nestled in the valley, a pungent odor that smelled like cat urine. The people of Bellehaven were used to it. They hardly noticed it anymore.

Today they welcomed the smell as if it were a gift from heaven, an honest-to-goodness miracle, because when the odor drifted through the tree branches, the crows lifted into the air, squawking their indignant protests, and headed west.

Nobody was as happy or relieved as Danny Giannetti, who barreled home from school, tires squealing as he made a sharp turn into the driveway. Without even bothering to change his clothes, he dragged the hose from the back of the house, got a bucket of hot soapy water, and began to scrub away more than four days' worth of crow droppings from his Mustang.

It was the first normal spring day since the previous Saturday when the four-day heat wave arrived, followed by the blizzard. The afternoon sun was warm. A light breeze swept the last of the dead leaves into the storm drain. Daffodils, buried under a half foot of snow two days before, their stalks bent to the ground, struggled to straighten up. Their stems, like hunched spines, swayed precariously in the breeze. Danny noticed none of this. His attention was on his Mustang.

The spray from the hose as it hit the car left dark splotches on his jeans and olive green T-shirt. He felt the sun on his neck, the wind in his hair, and for the briefest moment, he dared to hope. Nothing more had happened since the police confiscated Simon's computer on Tuesday. He was sure if there was something incriminating, the cops would have been pounding on his door by now, slapping handcuffs on him.

Danny shook his head as if trying to dislodge the image. He stepped back to admire his handiwork. The sight of the shiny black paint, the shimmering beads of water, reassured him. No crows cackled overhead. No crows threatened to undo his hard work. All was right with the world.

Until the image of Simon swirling the hose over his head suddenly popped uninvited into Danny's head.

Simon had come by Danny's house one Saturday morning in September, an hour before everyone was to hook up at Kyle's and head down to the school for the football game. Danny had been outside washing his new Mustang, his pride and joy, purchased with money earned from numerous after-school and summer jobs. He had the car stereo on full blast, ignoring the disgruntled remarks of his neighbors.

He had no idea why Simon had come by so early. He found his presence annoying and even a little disconcerting. Danny wanted to be left alone to wash his car in peace. It wasn't as if he and Simon were friends or anything. And without Kyle, Devin, and his other friends there, he didn't have a clue what to say to the little geek.

Simon slid inside the car on the passenger side and, to Danny's horror, began to switch stations. First to some country western station, then an oldies station.

Finally, after listening to some really boring classical piece, Danny had had enough. "What the hell's wrong with you, man?"

Simon blinked in surprise and pushed his glasses back up on his nose. "What?"

"What do you mean 'what?' I had it tuned to a decent station."

"Don't you ever listen to anything else?"

"Why should I?"

Simon shrugged. "I don't know. Just for the hell of it? Just to hear something different?"

"I like what I like," Danny said, unable to keep the irritation out of his voice. "Leave the damn radio alone." He stood there, looking outraged, as the sponge dripped soapy water down the front of his pants. "Jeez. Now look what you made me do."

Simon didn't look the least bit contrite. In fact, Danny noticed something in Simon's expression he hadn't seen before, although he couldn't put a name to it. The next thing he knew, Simon had sprung from the car, grabbed the hose, pressed the handle on the spray nozzle, and was spinning a stream of water over their heads like a lasso. Before he knew what hit him, Danny was soaked to the skin.

He lunged for the hose, shrieking obscenities at the top of his lungs, but Simon only laughed and continued to whip water over their heads. In no time flat, Danny was laughing too, smacking Simon with the soapy sponge.

Before they left for the game, Danny changed his clothes, but Simon, still dripping, his sneakers squishing and oozing water with each step, didn't bother. He told Danny he'd be dry before the second quarter, sitting out on those hot bleachers, and a whole lot cooler than everyone else. Danny thought Simon had a point and almost wished he hadn't changed his own clothes.

Now he lifted the hose from the driveway and stared down at the nozzle. The temptation to point it straight up in the air and swirl it the way Simon had was overwhelming. But it wouldn't be the same. Not without Simon.

Danny was busy smearing paste wax on the car, taking pride in each large swooping circle he made, when his sister, Marni, pulled into the driveway and parked her classic '65 T-bird right next to his car. She wore khaki hiking shorts and a pale orange T-shirt and held a Diet Pepsi in one hand. Danny spotted her grease-stained jeans tossed in a heap in the backseat and figured she must have changed at work.

She glanced at Danny's Mustang; then, shading her eyes with her hand, she squinted up at the treetops. "Thank god," she said. "If those damn crows were still here I was going to borrow Austin McAllister's BB gun and blast their feathers off."

Austin McAllister lived next door, and as far as Danny was concerned, he was a dorky little seventh grader with psychotic tendencies. On more than one occasion Danny had seen him sitting on his deck shooting at robins that settled on the branches of a black birch a few yards away. He was one of the few people Danny steered clear of.

"Nice talk," Danny said.

Marni shrugged and bent forward to check her reflection in the shiny surface of Danny's car. "Mrs. McCafferty is in the hospital." She ran her tongue over her lips to moisten them. "They're saying it could be that West Nile virus."

It took a few seconds for her words to register. Danny stood there with the can of paste wax in one hand and a rag in the other. "Devin's mom?"

"Her grandmother, I think." Marni straightened up and looked at him. "I told you. It's those damn crows. Ron Snyder, who heads the Mosquito Commission, was in to pick up his Pathfinder this afternoon. He says they found a dead crow in the McCaffertys' backyard and they're having it tested."

The hair on the back of his neck bristled, although he wasn't sure why that should be. He didn't even know Devin's grandmother, except to say hi in the A&P or when he saw her in town. "Did he actually say it's West Nile virus?"

"No. That's what some of the guys at the station are saying."

Danny smirked. "Oh, right. Yeah, like with their Ph.D.'s in biology, they've got it all figured out." This was a sore point with Marni and he knew it.

She took the bait. "Just because a person chooses not to go to some hotshot university doesn't mean they aren't smart." She spun around and headed toward the back door. "And there are plenty of stupid jerks who think because they're going to some snotty fancy school people won't notice they're brain-dead."

Danny laughed. He knew this was aimed at him, at his recent acceptance by Dartmouth. "It's too early for mosquitoes," he shouted to her back.

"Sorry, genius, but you don't know everything," she called over her shoulder. "Ron says all that rain we had at the end of March, followed by the heat wave that came through last Saturday, set off a mess of early hatchers." She bounced up the back steps and let the screen door slap shut behind her.

Danny went back to applying the paste wax, but the pleasure he'd felt earlier was gone. West Nile virus. So big deal, he thought. People got sick all the time. Only, for some reason, he couldn't shake a feeling of dread, the same feeling he'd had the morning the crows first descended on Bellehaven.

Kyle gently brushed Devin's hair away from her bowed head, trying to read her expression. They were standing inside the custodial closet, the same one Kyle and Danny had brought Simon to the day Kyle decided Simon would be Walter Tate's replacement.

"I thought you were going to drive me to the hospital," Devin said.

"I will, okay? After you talk to McCabe."

"I told my mom I'd be there right after school."

Kyle rolled his eyes and assumed his most patient look. "Dev, I know you're worried about your grandmother. I can understand that. But this computer security situation is definitely code blue. We have to move fast."

"Why can't you do it?" she said, looking up at him.

"McCabe's not about to tell me squat."

"So why should he tell *me* anything?" Devin took a step away from him. Her back was against the metal shelves.

How could he tell her it was because she was hot, because no guy could keep anything from her even if he tried? "It'll seem more innocent coming from you. You're just trying to find out about a friend who might be in trouble."

Devin twisted a loose button on her sweater. "You're better at getting what you want from people. I'm just going to blow it. I'll get nervous and screw it up."

"Dev, we've only got a short window of opportunity here. McCabe's still in the computer lab. If we don't move fast, we'll have to wait until Monday. I don't think we can afford to do that. Do you?"

Devin stared down at the button in the palm of her hand. She hadn't realized it had come off. She rubbed her thumb and forefinger over the smooth surface. Kyle was right, of course. They couldn't afford to wait.

A few minutes later, Devin stood outside the computer lab. The door was closed, which surprised her, but it wasn't locked. She opened it a crack and peeked inside. At the far corner of the room a bunch of seniors from the football team hovered over one of the computers. One of them let out a whistle. The others laughed.

Her heart was beating so fast she couldn't think straight. She had to be out of her mind to let Kyle talk her into this.

She was barely halfway into the room when she felt a hand on her shoulder. She spun around. She was face to face with Mr. McCabe. He frowned at her.

Scuffling sounds, the sounds of chairs being pulled out, and general clatter echoed behind her. Devin glanced over her shoulder. All the boys had suddenly taken seats in front of the other computers and seemed to be working. Vaguely she thought, Jocks? Computers? After school? It doesn't wash.

"You want something, Devin?"

Devin turned back to Mr. McCabe. She was momentarily distracted by the wild yellow and orange Hawaiian print shirt, buttons stretched to the limit across his bulging stomach. His red mustache was so thick and bushy, it hid his entire upper lip.

"Yes," Devin said, finally answering his question. "I need to talk to you." She looked over at the jocks. "Maybe this isn't a good time."

Mr. McCabe had assumed a more relaxed position. The frown had given way to a grin. A truly creepy grin, to Devin's way of thinking. "They're here for extra help," he said, nodding toward the group at the other end of the room. He shrugged and gave her a knowing look, as if to say, What do you expect, they're jocks, then steered her over to his desk and pulled up a chair for her.

"So, what's on your mind?" His voice was friendly enough, but Devin could see he was preoccupied. Every so often he shifted his eyes to where half the football team appeared to be working at the computers.

"It's about Simon," she said. She dropped her backpack next to the chair and sat down.

That got his attention. "Simon Gray?"

Devin nodded. "He's in trouble, isn't he?"

Mr. McCabe rested his elbows on his desk, linked his chubby fingers, and leaned forward. He took a deep breath, obviously stalling. "I'd say so. Being in a coma, that's—"

"I'm not talking about that," Devin said, trying not to sound impatient. "I mean, well, I heard something."

From the back of the room, one of the jocks yelled, "Hey, Mr. McCabe, my screen's frozen."

Looking as if the cavalry had arrived, Mr. McCabe got to his feet. He shoved his chair back with one leg. Devin knew if he retreated to the other side of the room, he could be there for a long time. Surprising even herself, she yelled to the boy, a senior named Alan Caldwell, to hit the Alt, Control, and Delete keys in sequence.

Alan stared at her for a minute, then shifted his gaze to Mr. McCabe. "Oh, yeah," he said. "Right. Forgot about that." He shrugged and stabbed his fingers at the keyboard.

"I just want to know if it's true," Devin said, before Mr. McCabe could escape. "Is he in trouble?"

"I'm not sure what kind of trouble you're talking about. What is this 'something' you heard?"

Devin swallowed hard. If she told him she knew about the breach of computer security, about the conversation he'd had with Dr. Schroder, Mr. McCabe would know she was somehow involved. "I heard the police came to his house and took his PC," she said.

"Who told you that?"

She had to think fast. Recalling what Charlie Atwater had told Danny, she said, "Simon's sister. She was at home when the cops showed up."

Mr. McCabe looked over at the jocks. He sighed. "Devin, I'm really not at liberty to discuss this case."

So it *is* a case, Devin thought. And McCabe was aware of it, which meant the investigation had gone beyond confiscating Simon's PC. The police were probably checking out the school computers as well.

"Maybe I can help?"

"Help how?" He was beginning to look annoyed.

"I don't know. Simon and I are friends. I know him pretty well."

"Do you know something about this?" He had sat down again, much to Devin's relief, and even looked interested.

"I know his sister," she said, dodging his question. This wasn't entirely true. She had met Courtney only a few times and had never really said more than hi to the girl. "Maybe I could talk to her, find out how much she knows. That's if I knew what to ask."

Mr. McCabe's frown returned. He had thick, bushy eyebrows the color of his mustache, which made the frown seem more menacing. "I'm sure the police have already questioned his sister to their satisfaction." He ran his hand through his hair. "Look, Devin, if you know something, I suggest you tell me. Otherwise, please don't waste my time. I have students who need my help."

Devin assumed he was referring to the jocks, most of whom, from what she could tell, didn't even seem to be working. They were talking and clowning around.

Mr. McCabe leaned back in his chair and folded his hands across his large belly. He eyed her suspiciously. "Just how much did Simon's sister tell you?"

Stupid stupid stupid. She was digging herself in deeper and deeper. Devin clutched the sides of the chair. All she'd been trying to do was find out how far the investigation had gone and if the police had found anything in the school computers. Or if they had other suspects. It seemed obvious that the investigation was still under way, and that was about all she'd discovered. It wasn't much to take back to Kyle, but she didn't know how to get any more information. She just wanted to leave.

Mr. McCabe was watching her. Waiting for her answer. "Not much, only about the police taking his computer. I thought you might know why." She bent over to pick up her backpack, then got up to leave. "It's like I told you, Simon's a friend. I was worried he might be in some sort of trouble."

"I'd worry more about whether he's going to come out of that coma," Mr. McCabe called after her as she headed for the door.

Her lame encounter with Mr. McCabe was a disappointment. Kyle wouldn't be too happy about how it had gone either. But what did he expect? She'd warned him she wasn't good at this Mata Hari stuff.

With the police involved, it could mean possible criminal charges for whoever was arrested. Right now it appeared Simon was their man. As far as she could tell, they weren't investigating anyone else. Not at the moment, anyway. So why did she feel so rotten?

Debra Santino opened the window behind her desk and stared down at the small mounds of melting snow by the curb in front of the county courthouse. They were almost black from the gravel and dirt heaped on them, magnets for gum wrappers, paper cups, garbage tossed from car windows and by pedestrians. The snow, dirt, and trash formed bleak sculptures—collaborative artistic efforts.

A cool spring breeze washed over the room, bringing welcome relief. She needed a clear head. It was late Friday afternoon and technically she had the weekend off. But she knew she would be in here again first thing Saturday and maybe Sunday. As long as it took.

On the desk in front of her was Simon Gray's PC. On the monitor was a poem. So far she had found dozens of poems and short stories on the boy's computer. Although these were not what she was looking for, she found herself reading them anyway, telling herself she might find a clue. Maybe one of the stories would be about a teenage hacker. But she knew that was unlikely. Simon didn't seem the type to leave such obvious evidence behind.

Over the past few days she had learned quite a bit about Simon Gray from Barbara Schroder, the principal of Bellehaven High. What she didn't understand was why Dr. Schroder wanted the police on this case. True, if it involved hacking, that would be a criminal offense. But Debra had handled enough of these cases in the public school system to know that one or more students had probably managed to get the teacher's password. Using someone else's password, while unethical, wasn't a crime.

She couldn't understand why Dr. Schroder didn't let George McCabe handle the situation. Not only was he the computer science teacher, he maintained the school's network. If anyone was in a position to search the log on the server for any suspicious activity, it would be McCabe. That way the school could keep this whole business under wraps. Debra had said as much to Barbara during their phone conversation a week earlier.

No one on the Bellehaven police force was trained to handle computer crimes. And the county did not have a computer crimes division. Ordinarily, if the police had to be involved, Lieutenant Santino, who worked in the county prosecutor's office, directed the problem to the High Technology Crimes and Investigation Support Unit in Trenton. But the situation at Bellehaven High didn't merit that kind of attention.

Barbara Schroder had called her not only because she had known Debra for years but because, as she told Debra, she was the most computer-savvy person in the county, with maybe the exception of Roger Garvey, a computer consultant who maintained the system in the prosecutor's office.

Debra hadn't missed George McCabe's obvious annoyance when she and Roger showed up at the school to download the server's log. And she couldn't blame him. There was no reason he couldn't handle the matter on his own.

But she had to admit, it was McCabe who had tipped her off about Simon Gray. He had told her that if anyone had the skill and knowledge to hack into the system or secure someone else's password, it was Simon. Although he'd quickly added that he couldn't imagine the boy doing such a thing. It wasn't in his nature.

Obviously there was more to Simon Gray than his knowledge of computers. Debra glanced at the monitor. A poem she had come across a few minutes earlier was still on the screen.

BAT WINGS

On nights with air so heavy a single breath
could drown us all

bats drink their fill of mosquitoes
swelling their bellies

on the graceful downswoop sail leeward,
their wings like shark fins, black on black,

invisible except for the brush
of air against the brow,

unlike us
their dark blades never
paperslice other wings
with bloodless cuts.

The lieutenant leaned back in her chair, staring at the screen. What was she to make of this? Did the "us" refer to people Simon Gray knew? Suddenly she was thrust back into her sophomore year of college and a literary analysis class she'd hated. The teacher, whose name she couldn't even recall, was always nagging her students to look beneath the surface of the stories they read, hinting they would find deeper meaning in the symbols, in the metaphors. It amused her to think her career as a police officer required her to do just that—look beneath the surface for what was rarely apparent at first glance. She wished now she had paid more attention in class.

Could the answers she was looking for be hidden somewhere in these poems, these stories? Maybe, but she needed to know more about the boy and his friends and family before she could make any connections.

And there was something else that bothered her: the accident. She wondered if it was possible that it wasn't an accident at all, wondered if Simon Gray had been desperate enough to attempt taking his own life. If that was the case, then what had made him that desperate? Had he committed a crime that could ruin his reputation, stain his permanent record? The question brought her back to where she had started—was Simon Gray a probable suspect or not?

Only an inch of thick lukewarm coffee remained in the glass pot of the coffeemaker. Lieutenant Santino sloshed it around, trying to decide whether to dump it and start another pot or just drink the sludge that was left. She would probably be there until late into the evening. So she opted to make a new pot of coffee. Then she went back to the computer sitting on her desk. Simon Gray's computer.

Later, when she reached for her coffee mug, the few swallows left were cold. As she got up to refill the mug, she glanced at her watch and saw that it was almost seven o'clock. She hoped her husband, Steve, had found something in the freezer to microwave, something he could make for himself and the girls. Well, it was too late to worry about that now, she thought, pouring another mug of coffee. She would call Steve in a few minutes.

But the few minutes turned into two more hours as she diligently opened documents within files that were tucked away within other files, hoping against hope that one of these documents would yield some sort of evidence.

The first thing Debra had checked, once she was able to access Simon's e-mail account, was his recent mail. The screen was blank. Not one e-mail remained, not even in his trash file. Not a shred of evidence. She would try to retrieve the messages later. But right now she searched his files, hoping to find some other revealing document, notes or letters, illegal software, or perhaps a journal.

If she couldn't find anything, she would turn Simon's computer over to Roger Garvey, who was currently going through the information they had downloaded from the school server, a daunting task, given the amount of data.

Both she and Roger suspected that whoever printed out the English test might have installed a keystroke recorder program they'd downloaded from the Internet, using it to record Abel Dodge's password when he logged on. It wouldn't be the first time someone had used such a program illegally. Lieutenant Santino was glad they had Roger working on the case. If there was anything suspicious in the server's log, Roger would find it.

In the meantime, she would keep prodding away at Simon's PC, because all her instincts told her there was something there. Something she normally wouldn't be looking for. Something that would give her a clue, something to go on, maybe even the evidence she needed. She didn't expect this to be easy, and she was willing to put in as much of her own time as necessary.

She knew from what George McCabe had told her that Simon Gray was bright. Knew he probably had a brilliant future ahead of him. Knew from questioning some of the other teachers and a few of Simon's neighbors that he was practically the poster boy for the perfect son, the one they all wished they had. And that was the problem, as far as she could tell. Simon Gray was just too good to be true.

Liz had spent all Saturday afternoon scrounging through stacks of dusty cardboard boxes in the basement of the building that housed the local historical society. She had all but given up when she pulled an old leather-bound book from one of the unmarked boxes. It had been buried beneath junk from someone's attic, or so Liz had decided—the kind of stuff you might find at a rummage sale. The leather binding was worn and cracked.

The overhead lights were so dim, Liz could barely make out the ink on the pages of what appeared to be someone's journal. On the first page, in elegant cursive and ink faded to a pale brown, were the words:

An Account of My Life from 1797 to 1800
by
Lucinda Alderman

If nothing else, this old journal, donated to the historical society along with countless other documents and objects by well-meaning families who wished to preserve their family history and its deep connections to the town of Bellehaven, was written during the time when the Wildemere trial and hanging took place. Liz ran her hand over the page, as if she could somehow make a connection with Lucinda Alderman.

Overhead, the muffled sound of crepe soles crossed the floor. The basement door opened and Mrs. Neidermeyer's gravelly voice floated down to her, alerting her that they would be closing the building in ten minutes.

Liz clutched the journal as if she expected Mrs. Neidermeyer to come tearing down the stairs and rip it out of her hands. After spending the entire afternoon in this musty basement, going through dirty boxes that had turned her fingers gray, she wasn't about to let her discovery be taken from her.

The upstairs rooms were already filled to overflowing, and it seemed unlikely that any of this stuff would ever see the light of day. At least not anytime soon, not until the society found a larger building. All these boxes of donated information had yet to be cataloged—mostly by senior citizens who volunteered their time. It would take years.

That was what Liz told herself as she unzipped her backpack and slipped the journal inside. Mrs. Neidermeyer would never allow her to take anything from the building. And the thought of waiting until Monday after school to read through this latest find, the only thing she'd discovered that was even remotely related to the period she was investigating, was agonizing. The journal had probably not even been cataloged. They would never miss it. She would return it in a few days, and no one would ever be the wiser.

Chapter 8

Simon had returned to the Liberty Tree. The streetlights cast eerie shadows on the road and sidewalk. At first he saw only a dark filmy cloud at the base of the oak. There was something familiar about the shape, something unsettling. But as hard as he tried to remember, he drew a blank.

The shape seemed to take on solid form, and that was when Simon realized he was staring at Jessup Wildemere. Again. Only now Jessup sat beneath the tree, his knees drawn to his chest, his head bowed, as if he were asleep. He wore the same clothes as before. Simon wasn't sure how much time had passed since their previous encounter. It seemed like only seconds since he'd last been there.

When Jessup looked up, Simon watched his expression change from hopeful to disappointed. He wondered if Jessup was still waiting for someone. "What are you doing out this time of night, lad?" Jessup asked.

"Nothing. Just walking." Simon didn't know what else to say.

Jessup held out his arm, pointing a finger at him. "In your nightshirt? And not much of a nightshirt at that." He laughed.

So Jessup Wildemere *could* see what he wore. Simon wondered why Jessup hadn't mentioned it before. Maybe he had been embarrassed for Simon and pretended he didn't notice.

"Sometimes I sleepwalk," Simon said. To his way of thinking, this answer wasn't all that far from the truth.

Jessup narrowed his gaze. He looked suspicious. "A body walking about while he sleeps?" He shook his head. "Sounds like the devil's work." Jessup got to his feet and brushed off the seat of his breeches. "Judging by those cuts and bruises on you, I'd say this sleepwalking is a dangerous pastime."

Simon didn't want to talk about his injuries. He wanted to leave this place. He didn't want to talk to Jessup Wildemere, because none of what was happening made sense. He had no rational explanation for these encounters, and that made him uneasy.

Jessup had taken a few steps away from the base of the tree. He stared up into the night sky. "Did you ever see so many stars?" he asked.

All Simon saw when he looked up were a few scattered stars blurred by the ground light. The windows in the Neidermeyer house were dark. But the fluorescent lights inside the Gulf station across the street were on. Curious, he nodded toward the station and asked Jessup what he saw.

Jessup scratched the back of his neck and stared in the direction Simon had indicated. "That's the road to the green," he said. He eyed Simon suspiciously. "Did you not tell me you were from around here?"

"What else do you see?"

"What else? Why, the western portion of Joseph Alderman's pasture, of course."

Simon had begun to understand this much: he and Jessup were standing in the same place, but not in the same time. They were somehow together in space but with more than two hundred years separating them. Everything around them, everything they saw, except for each other, was part of their own time. Neither could see what the other saw.

Nothing in Simon's experience or in his belief system had prepared him for such an incomprehensible situation. But then nothing had prepared him for the long blocks of time he spent in gut-wrenching pain in the empty dark, either. Yet as much as he hated being in the hospital, being here with Jessup Wildemere, in this haunted place, by this tree, was equally disturbing, but in a different way, although he couldn't explain why.

Simon closed his eyes and tried to will himself back into his body. But if there was one thing he had learned on these spontaneous out-of-body journeys, it was that he didn't seem to be in control of when they happened, where he ended up, or when he returned.

When he looked over at Jessup, the man was watching him with curiosity. Simon crossed the grass by the sidewalk and sat beneath the tree. The back of his head rested against the tar-coated gash. He remembered the conversation he'd had with Jessup during their last visit, and staring up at the figure standing next to him, he asked, "Didn't the person you were waiting for show up?"

A chill night breeze set the bare branches above them dancing. The glare of the streetlight covered the sidewalk and road in dappled, shimmering light. But no such light appeared on Simon, or on Jessup, whose face was bathed in the silvery blue light of a full moon, although Simon could see only a muted, cloud-covered moon in the sky. Jessup's gaze seemed far away. "She'll come," he whispered, more to himself than as a response to Simon's question.

Simon expected the ground beneath his thin gown to be cold and damp. But he felt nothing. And even there, outside, with the night air wafting about him, he could still detect the faintest odor of bleach.

He looked at the branches overhead and wondered which one Jessup Wildemere had dangled from the day the townsfolk hanged him. Did Jessup remember that day? Did he even know he was dead? Simon decided he wasn't going to be the one to break the news. If Jessup Wildemere thought he was alive, that was fine with Simon. As long as he wasn't stuck here with him for the rest of eternity.

Jessup reached into a leather pouch that hung from

his breeches and pulled out a small object. He hunkered down in front of Simon and opened his hand. The object was a ring with a dark green stone. It shone in a pool of moonlight in Jessup's hand. "It belonged to my mother," Jessup said. "My older brother, Samuel, inherited my father's farm when my father died last year. My mother wanted me to have something, too. So she gave me this when I left to strike out on my own. It belonged to her grandmother. It's a fine emerald, wouldn't you say?" Jessup gently rubbed his thumb back and forth over the green stone. "Do you think she'll like it?"

"Who?"

As if he were coming out of a trance, Jessup's head bobbed up. He blinked at Simon, stuffed the ring back into the leather pouch, and turned to look down Edgewood Avenue—although Simon knew Jessup didn't see a road there. Who could tell *what* he saw? Maybe woods. Maybe a path.

Simon felt the familiar tingling, the tug, and knew he was about to leave. He wanted to know whom Jessup was waiting for, whom the ring was for. But all he heard, before he was pulled back into his prison of flesh, was the hopeful echo of Jessup Wildemere's voice. "She'll be here. Before the moon falls beyond those treetops over there. You'll see, lad. You'll see."

The smell of bleach coming from the isolation room next to the one her grandmother was in made Devin gag. The nurses were disinfecting the room next door where a woman with a highly contagious, rare skin ailment had spent the past week.

Devin's grandmother was also in an isolation room and would remain there until the doctors could figure out what was wrong. Whatever she had could be contagious. Until they knew what they were dealing with, they weren't about to put her in with another patient. Devin had to wear a white mask that looped over her ears and covered her nose and mouth whenever she was in the room.

The day before, she had overheard two of the nurses whispering about West Nile virus, but as soon as they realized Devin was listening, they changed the subject. Devin had since checked out information on the virus on several Web sites. She knew if the virus developed into encephalitis people could die from it. Usually old people or those with weak immune systems. She was terrified for her grandmother.

That was why she was there. That, and because her mother, doing the fifty-yard dash around the kitchen table, stuffing Pop-Tarts into the toaster, plunking down cereal bowls in front of the six younger kids and getting everyone out the door to school, was feeling too shaky to drive that morning and had asked Devin if she'd mind missing school to take her to the hospital. It was on the tip of Devin's tongue to tell her mother she wouldn't mind missing school for the rest of the year, but all she'd said was "Sure. No problem."

Her grandmother moaned softly. Devin came to the side of the bed and stroked the woman's arm. Her grandmother had hair the color of Devin's, with only a few light streaks of gray. Her face and hands were freckled from gardening without a hat and gloves. During the heat wave, when anyone with any sense at all stayed indoors with the air conditioner running full blast, her grandmother had been outside raking soggy decayed leaves, turning soil, and mixing in mulch to prepare her flower beds.

Devin was suddenly reminded of the previous summer when she was a volunteer for Meals-On-Wheels. At first she hadn't thought it was in her nature to do that kind of volunteer work. Being around sick or extremely old people made her uncomfortable. But Kyle kept pushing her, saying volunteer work was just what colleges wanted to see on her application. To her surprise, she found she enjoyed bringing meals to people who were recovering from surgery or serious illness and to the elderly who had difficulty getting around. They were always so happy to see her, always begging her to stay for a cup of tea or oatmeal cookies.

Sometimes Simon rode along and helped her set up the meals. After a while, he didn't even have to look at Devin's list to know who was who. He remembered everyone's name.

As she stared at her grandmother's freckled hands, Devin thought of Mrs. Schollmeyer, who had been eighty-seven years old, had a weak heart, and lived alone in one of the large Victorian houses across from the park. When Simon and Devin brought her meals, she always sat by the side window in the living room so she could look out at her garden. Devin found the sight depressing. Weeds and brush had all but choked out the asters, strangled the delphiniums, and smothered the lavender. She couldn't bear to look. But Mrs. Schollmeyer always smiled out at the destruction as if it were the most beautiful sight on earth.

Then one Saturday, when Simon wasn't with her and Devin was setting up the small table by the window for Mrs. Schollmeyer, she looked up to see the loveliest garden she had ever set eyes on. It all but took her breath away.

Mrs. Schollmeyer, who had been sitting in the chair watching her, reached for her hand and gave it a gentle squeeze. "Your friend did this," she said. "Every day he came after school and weeded for me." She smiled, showing yellow teeth. "And he never charged a penny. Not a *penny.*" She squeezed Devin's hand hard for emphasis.

Mrs. Schollmeyer died three weeks later of heart failure, and Devin missed her. But maybe not as much as Simon did, although he never said so.

Devin's eyes filled with tears as she lifted her grandmother's limp hand and pressed it to her cheek. When her mother returned from the gift shop downstairs, Devin would head down to the intensive care unit and ask about Simon.

A few minutes later Mrs. McCafferty showed up at the door in skintight jeans and a V-neck T-shirt the color of the night sky, holding a small flower arrangement. She slipped on the mask that hung around her neck, then set the flowers on the single shelf by the closet. "That should cheer her up, don't you think?" she whispered and glanced over at the woman sleeping in the hospital bed.

Devin nodded as she watched a few of the daisy petals drift to the floor. She got up to give her mother the only chair, stepped into the hall, and removed her mask. "I'm going down to the cafeteria for coffee," she said. She had no idea why she didn't tell her mother the truth, tell her she was going to ask about Simon. She wondered if maybe she had gotten used to keeping secrets, even when it wasn't necessary.

Two administrative assistants looked up when Devin came through the double doors of the ICU. Three nurses were at the back of the room at the nurses' station. No way was she going to be able to sneak in to see Simon. So she approached the nurses, looking as respectful as she could.

For what seemed like several minutes, she stood quietly waiting for someone to notice her. When the youngest of the three women got up from the computer, she spotted Devin.

"Can I help you?" she asked.

Devin gave her a friendly smile and nodded. "I just want to inquire about someone. Simon Gray?"

"Are you a family member?" The nurse glanced at an older woman, who was putting medication into tiny white cups. Devin recognized her as the same nurse who had hustled Kyle and her out of Simon's room the week before. The woman looked at the younger nurse, then at Devin. Devin knew it was pointless to lie. From the look on the older nurse's face, she could tell the woman recognized her.

"No. I'm a friend."

The young nurse had long dark hair pulled back in a tortoiseshell clip and large, expressive eyes. Sympathetic eyes, Devin thought. But all she could tell Devin was that Simon's condition remained the same.

"Is he going to recover?"

Devin didn't miss the look the nurses exchanged. She knew they weren't about to say anything negative or discouraging, no matter how true it might be. Not to her, anyway. So she wasn't at all surprised when the younger nurse gave her what was meant to be a reassuring smile and said, "I'm sure he'll be fine."

In the smaller of the two waiting rooms around the corner from the ICU, Devin sank into a chair. She wasn't ready to go back to her grandmother's room. She was feeling oddly light-headed. She hadn't eaten much of anything since her grandmother became ill and she suspected, hoped, this was the reason for the dizziness.

But lately, ever since the day she had sought refuge in the dressing room at the Gap and found she couldn't make herself leave—at least not until Liz pulled her to her feet and propelled her through the louvered door—she had had trouble taking a single breath, as if the air would only go into her lungs just so far, then refused to go any farther. The harder she tried to breathe, the more light-headed she felt. She had almost passed out in calculus on Friday.

Feeling dizzy wasn't the only reason she chose to sit in this particular waiting room. She needed to be close to Simon. If she could, she would be in the ICU with him right that moment. She couldn't do a thing about what was happening to him. Still, it seemed important to be there.

The clock above the door read 11:30. She wondered what the others were doing right now. Ordinarily she would be in art. Kyle would be in calculus. On any other day when the bell rang, Kyle would head straight down the hall to the art room and wait outside the door so they could walk to the cafeteria together. Only, today she wouldn't be meeting him. She tried to imagine the expression on his face when she didn't come out of the classroom. Kyle hated surprises. He was a creature of habit. He thrived on order and routine.

So much had happened since her grandmother became ill, so much time was spent at the hospital and helping to take care of the other kids for her mother, that Devin could hardly remember what day it was. She hadn't even showed up for the last three play rehearsals, which all but guaranteed that her understudy would be playing the part of Lady Macbeth on opening night. Devin couldn't have cared less. She no longer wanted the role.

She hadn't seen Kyle since Friday, when he had insisted she talk to Mr. McCabe, hadn't talked to him since she called from the hospital Saturday afternoon to break their date. Until now, she really hadn't thought of Kyle at all over the weekend.

Not only hadn't she thought of Kyle, she hadn't missed him, not the way she'd always imagined she would if they broke up or if he moved away. Her lips parted with this startling revelation. She hadn't missed him at all. Not the least little bit. The person she missed, more than she had ever expected to, was Simon Gray.

By Monday afternoon, Liz had resolved to see Simon no matter what she had to do. She could tell by Courtney's heavy sigh and brusque "Nothing's changed," each time she called to ask about Simon, that Courtney was tired of her daily phone calls. Liz needed to see Simon for herself. If Kyle and Devin could sneak in, so could she.

After school, she headed straight home, borrowed the car keys from her mother under the pretext of doing research for her history paper at the library at the community college, and drove to the hospital.

She knew from what Devin had told her that it wouldn't be easy to get inside the intensive care unit undetected. The good news, as Liz saw it, was that Simon's room was the second on the left, right inside the doors. And according to Devin, the nurses kept the curtain drawn across the glass wall. How hard could it be to slip in there? She would have to move fast, pick the right moment, but she didn't doubt for a minute she could pull it off.

At the hospital, as she walked past the glass wall of the cafeteria, she spotted Mr. Gray sitting alone at one of the tables drinking coffee. An uneaten sandwich sat on the plate in front of him. That was a good sign. It meant it would probably be a while before he returned to Simon's room.

Courtney was not in her usual spot in the cramped waiting room when Liz peered inside the door. She thought Courtney might be in Simon's room, so she waited for ten minutes. When no one came out of the ICU, Liz decided Courtney hadn't come to the hospital yet.

A telephone hung on the wall right outside the two adjoining waiting rooms. Below it were a small desk and chair. Liz positioned herself in the chair and pretended to be looking up a number in the phone book. From this spot, she could see anyone walking toward the doors of the ICU. Her chance arrived in the form of a nurse and two men in khakis and blue polo shirts, wheeling a patient on a gurney. One man managed the patient's respirator, the other the IV pole. The nurse pressed the circular metal plate and the doors thumped open.

Liz found it surprisingly easy to follow this busy cluster of activity into the ICU and slip through the second door into Simon's room.

At first she thought she was in the wrong room. Simon looked so different, she hardly recognized him. Blue-black smudges circled his closed eyes. His lips were swollen, and there were all those tubes and machines fighting to keep him alive. The bruises on his face had turned a greenish yellow.

Forcing herself to focus on why she had come, she reached for his hand. She had read somewhere that people in a coma could still hear. So she leaned close to him and whispered, "Simon. It's Liz."

She looked around for a chair. There was only one in

the room. She placed it next to the bed. Then she reached through the side rail and lifted Simon's hand again. She had no idea what to say. How did you bring someone back from a coma? What if he didn't want to come back? This thought hadn't occurred to her until now. But remembering the way Simon had behaved the Saturday before the accident made her curious about what had really happened the night he skidded into the Liberty Tree. She didn't want to believe for a minute he would do such a thing on purpose. He would have left a note, right? He wouldn't just leave everyone to wonder. You had to have a reason for taking your own life. *Did you have a reason, Simon? Something you couldn't tell me?*

Liz didn't say this out loud. Instead she whispered, "Can you feel me holding your hand?" She ran the tips of her fingers along his palm. "Can you move your fingers? Even a little? Just one finger?" She stared down at their hands, hers gently cupping his. Nothing happened.

"Look, I know last Saturday you were really upset about something. You didn't want to talk about it, remember?" She paused and stared down at his hand again, hoping for some sign that he'd heard her. Still nothing.

"Whatever it is, Simon, it can't be so bad you wouldn't come back to us, right? I mean, your dad and Courtney, they've been here every day. And you've got lots of friends who are worried sick. They care about you." She paused to take a breath. "I care about you," she whispered.

Liz was so intent on getting through to Simon that she didn't hear the soft padding of the nurse's white sneakers coming across the floor until it was too late.

"This is an intensive care unit, miss. Immediate family only." The nurse, who wasn't much older than Liz, wore white slacks, a white tee and a colorful overblouse. Her brown hair was pulled back and held with a tortoiseshell clip.

"I'm his sister," Liz told her. "Courtney." Even Liz knew how pitifully unconvincing she sounded.

The nurse looked sympathetic. "I've met Simon's sister," she said. She glanced up at the monitor, then back at Liz. "I'm sorry, but you'll have to leave."

Liz was standing now. As she slid her hand from Simon's she felt the lightest touch. His forefinger had brushed her palm, a touch so slight she couldn't be sure she hadn't imagined it. "Did you see that?" She turned to the nurse, who was going over the chart in her hands.

"See what?"

"I think his finger moved." Liz tried to suppress the excitement in her voice. She didn't want to get her hopes up.

The nurse looked interested. She came to the side of the bed and touched Simon's hand. Then she took his pulse.

Despite herself, Liz felt a twinge of jealousy. She wanted to leave Simon with *her* touch. She knew it was ridiculous, but she couldn't seem to help herself.

"It might have been a reflex action," the nurse said. "That's not uncommon." She looked over at Liz. "I'll tell his doctor." For the first time she smiled at Liz. "You'd better get yourself out of here before anyone else sees you," she said.

Fifteen minutes later Liz was driving up over the hill

into Bellehaven when she suddenly noticed thousands of crows lined up on the telephone and power lines like dark soldiers awaiting her return. She rolled down the car window and sniffed the air. The wind had shifted. The cat urine smell from the pharmaceutical plant was gone. And the crows had come back. With a vengeance.

Her heart began to pound wildly. She felt as if the birds were following her. She stepped on the gas and tore down Edgewood Avenue at twenty-five miles over the speed limit. As if she were running a gauntlet, she kept her head so low her chin almost touched the steering wheel. The birds swooped toward the car, missing the windshield by inches. Their claws scratched across the car roof, the sound of fingernails on a blackboard. Their shrill caws beat against her eardrums.

Even while she struggled to keep her sweating palms from slipping off the steering wheel as she turned onto her street, even while she tried to focus all her concentration on pulling into the driveway and making it through the front door safely, some small part of her was only now beginning to understand that the crows wanted something from her—wanted something, perhaps, from everyone in Bellehaven.

Debra Santino was digging out the last noodle from her cup of microwaved chicken soup when she noticed an unnamed document on Simon's PC in a folder called SummerJobs. She had been in this folder before, knew it contained several drafts of Simon's résumé and letters to computer camps inquiring about openings. All on the up-and-up. Nothing suspicious. But she couldn't remember if she had opened this document with the default name doc2.doc before or not, and so clicked on it.

This, too, appeared to be a draft of an incomplete letter. But there was no address, no name, only the initial *D* at the beginning. And it was obvious from the first sentence that the letter had nothing to do with Simon's quest for a summer position. Debra scanned the letter, pausing to reread the last few lines.

> ***. . . Why do you think I let K and D talk me into this mess? For you. That's the only reason. Why else would I put everything I've worked for at risk? I have everything to lose and only one thing to gain, only one thing I really***

The letter stopped abruptly, right in the middle of Simon's thought. The lieutenant could almost feel his hopeless frustration, almost hear him thinking, What's the point?

Her spoon made a loud clatter as she dropped it into the empty cup. She was just beginning to understand that Simon had made a mistake. He probably never intended to save this document. He'd been pouring out his heart, sharing his deepest feelings in a letter he'd never planned to send. She could imagine him clicking on the *X* to close the file and then accidentally clicking on *YES* instead of *NO* when asked if he wanted to save the document. So what was this letter doing in his SummerJobs folder?

After wrestling with this question for a few minutes, the lieutenant refilled her coffee mug and checked the date on which this partial letter had been written. Then she looked to see if any other documents had been created in that file on the same day. Sure enough, another letter, one written to a computer camp in Massachusetts, was dated March fifteenth, the same day as the letter to the mysterious D.

All this time, as she searched through files, using key words, words like *project, PC, hack,* and the names of Simon's friends—a list put together after talking with his teachers and family—here was this obscure unnamed document, accidentally saved in the folder Simon happened to be in at the time he wrote it. Because he had used initials rather than names, and vague terms like *mess* and *risk,* the search-and-find mission hadn't been successful.

Debra read the unfinished letter several times. She wondered if somehow the "mess" Simon referred to also had to do with some of the kids on her list of his friends. The D to whom the letter was addressed might refer to Devin McCafferty. The K, to Kyle Byrnes, the other D, Danny Giannetti, perhaps. So far, she had not questioned any of the students at Bellehaven High. It had been important to keep the suspicions of the school officials under wraps to avoid alarming other potential suspects into destroying evidence.

Debra leaned back in her chair, lifted her coffee mug, took a swallow of the now lukewarm liquid, and reread the last fragment of Simon's letter. She was having second thoughts. She was beginning to think this might be a good time to start questioning Simon's friends, especially the three hinted at in the letter. She was just now entertaining the idea that even if Simon Gray was the brains behind the operation, he might not be in this alone.

Chapter 9

Kyle was coming out of Principal Schroder's office as Devin came through the door. His mother, a short overweight woman in baggy slacks and a purple tunic top, was right behind him. Devin wanted to ask him what this was all about, assuming they'd been called to the office for the same reason, but Kyle brushed past her with barely a nod. Mrs. Byrnes, however, gave her a sympathetic smile and said she felt "just awful" about Simon's accident.

"He's such a great kid, you know?"

Devin avoided looking at Kyle, although she knew he was watching her. She nodded. "Yeah, he is. Great kid." As she turned to go into Dr. Schroder's office, she sneaked a glance at Kyle, who remained expressionless. She knew him well enough to know this was his way of saying, Play it cool. Keep your guard up.

Principal Schroder sat behind her desk, sifting through manila folders. Devin noticed how every iron gray hair had been teased to within an inch of its life and sprayed into place. The woman could walk through a wind tunnel and not a hair would move. When Dr. Schroder found the file she wanted, she passed it over to a younger woman, a person Devin had never seen before. The woman, wearing khaki slacks and a pinstripe oxford blouse, had short dark hair, light freckles, and serious gray eyes that seemed to see right through Devin. She glanced at the contents of the folder, then nodded to Principal Schroder, who told Devin to take a seat. Principal Schroder smiled at her, but Devin didn't feel the least bit reassured.

In all her years of high school, she had never been in this office, a surprisingly friendly room with hanging plants, cheerful print curtains, and dozens of fascinating little objects like the clear glass paperweight sitting on the desk. Frozen in the center of the glass were a pansy and a bee.

As she slipped into the chair in front of Dr. Schroder's desk, Devin found she couldn't take her eyes off that poor bee. It was scarcely a quarter inch from the flower, yet doomed never to land on it, never to drink the sweet nectar.

"This is Lieutenant Santino, Devin," Dr. Schroder said. "She works in the county prosecutor's office. If you don't mind, she has a few questions she'd like to ask you."

Devin's heart plunged into the pit of her stomach like

a rock hitting water. She pulled her eyes from the bee and stared at the principal as if the woman had just asked her to do a swan dive from the George Washington Bridge. Devin's legs began to twitch, a nervous habit she had. She pressed the palms of her hands on her knees, hoping it wasn't obvious. Fine beads of sweat broke out on her upper lip and forehead. From the corner of her eye she could see Lieutenant Santino studying her.

Dr. Schroder leaned forward and folded her hands in front of her. "It's school policy to have a parent present whenever a student is questioned by the authorities. But we haven't been able to reach either of your parents." She paused. And Devin realized she was waiting for an explanation.

"My dad's on the road. He's a truck driver. Mom's at the hospital. Gram's not well."

Dr. Schroder looked sympathetic. "I'm sorry to hear that." She lifted a pen and began tapping the end against her other hand. The gesture made Devin even more nervous.

"The questions aren't actually related to you, Devin. They're about another student. You certainly aren't in any trouble. So if you don't have any objections, perhaps you can answer a few questions for Lieutenant Santino. But we'll certainly understand if you decline."

Devin tried to swallow but found she couldn't. "No . . . I mean, it's okay," she said, keeping her focus on Dr. Schroder.

"I appreciate this, Devin," Lieutenant Santino said, resting part of her backside on the corner of Dr.

Schroder's desk, one foot pressed to the floor for balance, the other dangling. She glanced down at the folder, then smiled at Devin. "I see you're an excellent student." She waved her hand over the open file. "These are some fine schools you've been accepted to."

It was all Devin could do just to nod. For all Dr. Schroder's reassurances, Devin was afraid this interrogation was going to be about the stolen passwords and wished the woman would just get on with it.

Lieutenant Santino closed the folder and put it on the desk. "How well do you know Simon Gray?"

Devin's legs began to twitch again. She crossed them at the ankles, pressing hard to keep them from moving. She shrugged, buying time. She decided the lieutenant probably already knew the answer to this question, knew Simon was part of their group. If Devin lied, it could make things worse. "He hangs out with us sometimes."

"Us?"

"Me and some other friends."

"So would you say you all have things in common?"

"Not necessarily. We've been hanging out since we were in middle school."

"Simon, too?"

"No. I meant the others."

"So when did Simon start hanging out with your group?"

There was a good chance Lieutenant Santino had already asked Kyle or maybe some of their other friends this question. Devin wondered if the police had been able to determine when Simon first began using teachers' passwords to get into the system. If they had, they might have already figured out that the date correlated pretty closely to when he began hanging out with her and the others. But then, there had been Walter first . . . so maybe . . . "I don't remember," she said. "It seems like he's always been around, sort of on the fringe." This last part was true, to Devin's way of thinking. She hadn't thought about it before, but looking back, it seemed as if Simon was never all that far away from her, waiting on the sidelines.

"Has he ever talked to you about things he's interested in?"

Devin dug her nails into her kneecaps. "Some people think all he cares about are computers and all that techie stuff. But they're wrong." She met the lieutenant's eyes head-on. The lieutenant's eyebrows arched slightly. Devin was afraid she might have sounded too defensive. If Lieutenant Santino suspected Devin knew why she was questioning her, she might conclude that Devin was aware of Simon's illegal computer activities. Or worse—was a part of them. Still, it seemed important to let the lieutenant know Simon was more than some computer nerd.

"He's into a lot of stuff. Old movies. Jazz. He likes going to plays at the McCarter Theatre. We saw *Agamemnon* there last fall." Devin remembered how Simon, who had the same English teacher, had talked his way into getting to come along, even though the trip was for seniors. "He's got this thing about Greek tragedy." Devin looked away. She was talking way too much.

"So Simon likes the theater?"

"Well, yeah. I mean, maybe it's not what most kids are into, but Simon's got his own interests. I mean, he actually *likes* Shakespeare. He tried out for a part in our school play this year. We're doing *Macbeth.*" Devin pressed her lips together, aware, suddenly, that she was practically babbling, telling this person far more than she'd intended. Lieutenant Santino didn't need to know Devin had landed the lead female role and then had blown it by not attending rehearsals.

"And did Simon want to play Macbeth?"

Devin tried to decide what Lieutenant Santino was looking for. Did she find that funny: a skinny, pale kid playing the role of a ruthless king? Did she think it wasn't possible?

"He wanted to be one of the ghosts." Devin knew she sounded defensive, but she couldn't seem to help it. She didn't like this woman prying into their lives.

"Really?"

"Yes, *really,*" Devin said. She told herself to calm down. What was she getting so uptight about? She leaned against the back of the chair, folded her arms across her chest, and tried to rearrange her expression into something between pleasant and noncommittal. She didn't need to piss off the lieutenant right now.

"Did he say why he wanted that particular part?"

Devin thought she knew the answer to this, but didn't see any reason to tell the lieutenant. It was none of her business. "No," she said. She shifted uneasily in the hard chair. She was thinking about what Simon had said when she had asked him the same question, the afternoon the two of them went to Alfonso's on Main Street for pizza after tryouts. He'd only grinned at her, a small blob of pizza sauce on his chin, and said, "Macbeth's a haunted man. I'd rather be the one doing the haunting than the other way around, wouldn't you?"

Lieutenant Santino watched Devin with interest.

"Anyway, what does it matter?" Devin told her. "He didn't get the part."

After a few minutes of uncomfortable silence, the lieutenant said, "So you'd say Simon Gray was a fairly interesting guy? Well-rounded. Not exactly what you kids call a geek."

"He's no geek," Devin informed her. "And yes, he *is* interesting. In his own way." Devin thought she understood what Lieutenant Santino was trying to do. She was trying to make it seem as if Simon wasn't the type of kid Devin and her friends would hang out with. That might mean they had another reason for letting him tag along—namely exploiting his computer skills. But she wasn't about to let this woman trick her into giving anything away.

"It says in your file that you're thinking of majoring in psychology."

Devin didn't have a clue where this was going. It wasn't what she was expecting to hear next. And since the lieutenant's comment wasn't really a question, she sat tight. Waiting.

"Do you ever use the Internet for your research?" the lieutenant asked.

"Doesn't everybody?"

"Would you consider yourself fairly knowledgeable about computers?"

Devin stared down at her folded arms. "I don't know. Not really. I know how to find information, send e-mails, use it to write papers, things like that. Same as most kids in the school."

"Did Simon help you when you had computer problems?"

"Yeah, he did. I was always messing up, losing files, deleting things accidentally. Sometimes my monitor would freeze up. Or I'd get these weird error messages."

"Did he help your other friends?"

"You mean if their computers were giving them grief?" Devin shrugged. "I guess. I never asked him."

"Did he ever help you with anything else?"

Devin felt a warm flush creeping up her neck to her face. She shot a look at Principal Schroder. "What's this about, anyway? Is Simon in trouble or something?" The principal looked momentarily caught off guard, which was what Devin had intended. Then, before either woman could respond, Devin said, "I can see why you wanted my parents here." She shoved her hair behind her ears and shook her head. "Simon's a friend. What if I say something wrong, even if it's an innocent remark? What if . . . Does his dad know about this little inquisition?"

Principal Schroder's lips parted as if she was going to say something, then snapped closed again.

"As Dr. Schroder said, you don't have to answer anything you don't want to," Lieutenant Santino informed her. "It's just that Simon Gray, as you know, is in a coma.

We're trying to find out as much about the accident as possible. Putting together a personality profile based on what friends and family tell us could be useful."

"Useful, how?" There wasn't a doubt in Devin's mind what this woman was really after. She was using the accident as a cover.

"Sometimes these cases—accidents—aren't really accidents."

"Are you saying someone tried to kill Simon?"

Lieutenant Santino left her seat on the desk and moved across the room to the window. Her back was to Devin. "Not at all."

"You think he ran into that tree on purpose? That's crazy. He'd never do that."

"Hopefully not," the lieutenant said. "In any case, you've been very helpful. If you think of anything else that may shed some light on Simon's accident, I'd appreciate it if you'd let Dr. Schroder know."

As Devin was leaving Principal Schroder's office, she heard someone call her name and looked up to see Danny sitting in the row of seats by the wall across from the secretary's desk. His father was with him. Danny looked worried. But with Angela Beckett blatantly watching them, Devin didn't dare so much as hint at what was to come. She only hoped Danny could keep his cool and wouldn't let Lieutenant Santino trip him up.

After school, as he pulled out of the school parking lot, Danny spotted two vans for a local news team cruising down Edgewood Avenue. The first thing he thought of was that they'd come to report on the story about the breach of computer security at the high school. Maybe they wanted to be right there at the scene when the police rounded up the suspects. Or whatever it was they were going to do.

If he went home, the cops might already be waiting for him. This wouldn't have surprised him in the least, not after the interrogation Lieutenant Santino put him through a few hours earlier. All those questions about Simon, trying to make Danny think this investigation was about the accident. He hadn't bought any of it. He knew Lieutenant Santino was looking for something else, could tell she was waiting for him to screw up.

And then there was Devin, coming from Dr. Schroder's office as he waited outside with his dad. So it wasn't just him. That much was obvious. Santino was checking out the whole group, maybe even their friends who weren't in on "the project."

Instead of going home, Danny headed for the river and parked his Mustang near the boat ramp. He did his best thinking at the river. Usually when he was fishing. But he didn't want to risk going home for his rod, even though trout season had opened a few days before and he was sorely tempted.

The Delaware was swollen with the runoff from Wednesday's snow and bulging with trout. It was close to overflowing its banks. Low branches, bending into the water, were being pummeled to the breaking point. The trees were black with noisy crows.

Danny eyed them nervously. He was angry as hell about their return, but he figured there wasn't a whole lot he could do about it. And he sure wasn't about to let them dictate where he could hang out. He pulled his sunglasses from his pocket, slipped them on, and sat on the ground, leaning back against a pine tree. He didn't notice the sticky sap seeping into his shirt, although he was aware of the pungent smell.

He was staring up at the narrow metal bridge a few hundred yards away that linked New Jersey and Pennsylvania, worrying about the cops and thinking how easy it would be to walk across the bridge into another state, when Kyle showed up.

"I figured you'd be down here," Kyle said. He parked himself on a flat rock near the riverbank.

Danny squinted at him through his sunglasses and waited.

"Santino talk to you this morning?" Kyle asked.

"Yeah, so? She talked to Devin too."

"And me."

The crows overhead had grown silent, except for the occasional rustling of their wings. Danny had the eerie feeling they were eavesdropping. "Anybody else? I mean, was it just the three of us she questioned or some of the others in the posse?"

"Just the three of us, as far as I can tell."

"Why just us three? How could she know?"

Kyle pulled his legs up and circled them with his arms. His sneakers glinted pure white in the sunlight. Danny couldn't figure out how anyone could keep their sneakers looking that clean. "Maybe she'll talk to the others later," he said. But Danny could see that Kyle didn't really believe that.

"That was all bullshit about Simon's accident, right?" Danny leaned forward, feeling the pull of the sticky bark on his hair. "Trying to make us think he might have done it on purpose, running into that tree."

"She was trying to find out how much we know, without letting on what this investigation is really about." Kyle picked up a flat stone and skipped it several yards along the surface of the river.

"You think she knows about the project?"

Kyle shook his head. "She probably isn't even sure about Simon. I think she's just grasping at straws."

"What if they've found something on his computer?"

"Then they'll have to talk to Simon about that." Kyle snickered and skipped another rock.

Danny stood up and walked over to the edge of the river. He watched the water beating against the muddy bank. "Who knows what Simon's going to do when he comes out of this coma? Maybe this whole accident thing will have him all freaked and ready to confess damn near anything."

"Who says he's coming out of the coma?"

Danny looked down at Kyle's upturned, expressionless face. "Why wouldn't he?"

"From what I saw of that accident, man . . . He was really messed up. Even if he lives, which I sort of doubt, his brain might not function the same."

"You mean, like a permanent veg-out?"

"Something like that."

Except for those first few panicky minutes after Kyle had called to tell him about the accident, Danny had fully expected Simon to pull through. He couldn't bring himself to believe that Simon might not recover from the coma, or if he did, that he could end up a vegetable. Danny had never known anyone his own age who had died. Simon was a kid, for god's sake. A year younger than he was. He had his whole life ahead of him.

"He could still make it," Danny said, surprised by the level of defiance in his voice.

Kyle got to his feet and came to stand by Danny. He had his hands in his pockets; he looked thoughtful. "That's not exactly in our best interest, you know."

Danny looked away. This wasn't something he wanted to think about. "Well, there's not a whole lot we can do about it."

Kyle nodded and looked out at the river. "Maybe. Maybe not."

Danny felt a chill run along his spine. There was something about the matter-of-fact tone in Kyle's voice that disturbed him. Danny looked up at the branches overhead, limbs bent to the breaking point with the weight of hundreds of crows. He tried to think of what he would do if Simon recovered and decided to spill his guts, but he came up empty-handed. He turned to Kyle. "So what do we do?"

Kyle shrugged. "The way the system works, as far as I can see, is you can do just about anything you want. The trick is, you have to make sure no one ever finds out."

"And if they do?"

"You lie like hell."

"Meaning?"

"They think Simon's their man. We just need to make sure all the evidence points to their prime suspect and no one else. Being good Bellehaven citizens, it's our civic duty to help the police in any way we can, right?"

Danny couldn't believe what he was hearing. Was Kyle suggesting they frame Simon?

Kyle turned to leave, then stopped a few feet away and looked back at Danny, who stood gaping at him in disbelief. "Face it, man. It'll be a lot easier for all of us if he just stays in a coma."

Simon was surprised to find himself standing on the bank of the Delaware in broad daylight, watching the churning brown water, water so muddy it resembled a pot of boiling hot chocolate. The water gouged the riverbank, carving out chunks of mud as it charged along, pulling at low branches, exposing roots.

He wasn't sure why he'd come here instead of the Liberty Tree. He'd sensed unfinished business there, in that other place.

The sound of rocks hitting water drew his attention. Simon turned to see Danny sitting beneath a pine tree. Kyle sat a few feet away, tossing stones into the water. The spot where they sat, even the tree Danny leaned against, was familiar. Simon himself had come to this place many times, when he wanted to get his head straight. But something was different about it that day. Maybe it was the thousands of crows lurking in the bare branches, along the river's edge. Black feathers in place of leaves. Or maybe it was the muted, almost mournful caws they murmured, so unlike their usual barking cackles. The sound cut right through him. He felt a tingling in his fingers and on the back of his neck. This place had begun to remind him of something disturbing, although he couldn't remember what.

Kyle and Danny were leaving. Kyle was already several yards ahead of Danny, heading toward the parking lot by the boat ramp. Simon called to them. He reached out to grab Danny's arm as he passed within a foot of him. But Danny kept right on walking. He didn't see Simon.

Right then Simon would have given anything to be able to talk to him. To anyone, for that matter. Especially Liz. He had started to follow Danny when a crow suddenly landed on his shoulder. Simon was so startled he let out a yell. The crow threw back its head and cackled, a strange kind of bird laughter. That was when Simon realized that the bird not only saw him, but heard him. As Stanley Isaacson had; as Jessup Wildemere had. He wondered if the bird, like him, was invisible. Surely people fishing along the river would find it odd to see a bird perched so securely in midair, its talons curled around nothing.

All about him, thousands of crows called from the branches overhead, a chorus of replies to the bird on his shoulder. The bird cawed back and raised its wings. Black feathers brushed the side of Simon's face.

The crow lifted its wings, circled Simon, then swooped into the tall grass by the muddy bank, disappeared, and shot back into the air, a black rocket with something wriggling in its mouth.

When the crow came to roost again on Simon's shoulder, Simon saw it had a small frog in its beak. The frog's legs twitched in all directions at once in a frantic effort to swim from the crow's mouth.

Simon tried to help the frog, but his hand froze in midmotion each time he reached for the crow. And there was something else: his own arms and legs had begun to flail in frantic desperation. Hundreds of frogs were suddenly all over him. They crawled up his bare legs, sprang onto his arms, tangled their webbed feet in his hair. Searing pain coursed through his body. He had to escape. His heart beat so wildly it made him dizzy. He was sickened at the sight of the frogs. No. More than that, he was terrified. The frogs reminded him of something, something he couldn't run away from.

When Devin and her mother walked through the back door early that evening, their arms loaded with buckets of chicken from KFC, they found Kyle sitting at the kitchen table playing gin rummy with the twins, Michael and Noah. Devin couldn't have been more surprised if she'd discovered an elephant washing dishes at the kitchen sink. In the four years they'd been together Kyle had showed up at her front door only to pick her up for special events, like the junior prom. Otherwise, they met someplace else. Never once, in all that time, had he simply dropped by. Things were usually too chaotic at her house for Kyle's taste.

Her mother seemed as surprised as Devin. She set the tubs of chicken on the counter and stared at them. She looked doubtful. Devin knew her mother was wondering if she had enough to feed another mouth.

"Woo hoo!" Noah shrieked. He fanned out his cards and laid them on the table. "I'm out. Count 'em and weep."

Michael slapped his cards down in a rage. "You cheated. I saw you. You picked up two cards together last time."

Kyle gave Noah a light punch on the arm. "Never let them see your sleight of hand, Noah my man."

"That's your advice to a nine-year-old?" Devin said. "Don't get caught?"

"That's my advice to anyone."

Devin, who hadn't bothered to take off her fleece jacket, was out the back door in a flash. She had no idea where she was going. But she knew she couldn't stay in the house for another minute. It wasn't until she was halfway down Meadowlark Drive, walking so fast she was practically jogging, and had turned onto Spencer Avenue, heading toward the Delaware, that she realized it wasn't the house or her family she was running from this time. It was Kyle.

And within seconds of this discovery, she heard his sneakers slapping the sidewalk behind her.

"Where're you headed in such an all-fired hurry?" he said. He jogged along beside her.

Devin knew there was no way to outrun him now, so she slowed her pace. "I need to be alone, that's all."

"Right this minute?"

"Yes."

Kyle stepped in front of her and put his hands on her shoulders. "We need to talk."

"About what?"

"About what happened this morning, for one thing. About that Lieutenant Santino. Son-of-a—it was like some inquisition."

"For you, maybe," Devin said. "She asked me about Simon, that's all."

"Think about it. You, me, and Danny. As far as I can tell, we're the only ones she questioned. Now, how did she know to talk to us? Just us. No one else in the school talked with her."

"Someone probably told her we were Simon's closest friends, except maybe for Liz. Everyone at school knows he hangs out with us." For all her attempts to find a reasonable explanation, Devin was growing uneasy. Maybe Kyle had a point. But right now he seemed to be backing off. His expression was thoughtful.

"There's something else we need to talk about," he said. His voice softened. He sounded almost hesitant.

"So talk."

Kyle sighed and looked around. "Not here."

"Fine. The park, then." Devin shifted course and headed down Locust Street toward the park.

Kyle fell into step, protesting. "It's too public. We need to be alone."

Devin smiled in spite of herself. She knew what was coming. If they were alone he probably thought he could maneuver out of whatever the problem was with a few kisses. But Devin knew that wouldn't work anymore, even if Kyle hadn't figured it out yet. "It's dinnertime. No one will be in the park this time of night." She zipped up her jacket. The chill spring air was cooler than she had expected now that the sun had dropped behind the trees.

When they reached the park, Devin sat on one of the benches. As she had predicted, they were alone. Kyle stood in front of her. He didn't bother to sit down.

"I don't want to lose you," he said. He looked over her head at the houses across the street.

This was not what Devin had been expecting. Never once had she said anything about breaking up. Until that moment, she hadn't even let herself think about how she would go about it if she did break it off. Now, it seemed, she would have to make a choice, would have to tell him she didn't like what they'd become, that she didn't think she could continue seeing him. She was going to have to tell him this, and without any mental rehearsal. The palms of her hands grew damp. She rubbed them on her jeans. What could she say that wouldn't sound stupid or clichéd? They had been together four years.

Kyle was waiting for her response. He was looking straight at her now. Devin stared down at the ground.

The tears on her lashes spilled onto her cheeks. There was nothing to say. Somehow they both knew this. In the end, Kyle simply turned around and walked down the dirt path toward the other side of the park.

Devin watched his receding back, poker straight, hands stuffed in the pockets of his J.Crew cargo pants. She couldn't believe she'd actually broken up with him, hadn't even tried to work things out.

Long after Kyle had disappeared from sight Devin continued to sit on the bench, watching the sky deepen from violet to midnight blue, watching the lights come on and shades being drawn in the homes surrounding the park. She was still reeling from the rush of silence that had, without warning, swept Kyle right out of her life.

She thought of the day she and Liz had gone to the Gap, how she had sought refuge in the dressing room only to find herself face to face with a stranger when she looked in the mirror. But until now there had been Kyle. When she was with him, she could almost make herself believe she was still the same person. Now that thin veil of self-deception was gone. Kyle had taken it with him, leaving her with only a numb emptiness.

Chapter 10

By Wednesday nine cases of West Nile virus had been diagnosed among the residents of Bellehaven. In a town of fewer than two thousand, this was considered an epidemic. No one, least of all the people at the county health department, could figure out why the virus seemed, for the moment anyway, to be isolated in this tiny out-of-the-way town on the bank of the Delaware. The last town in New Jersey—as one reporter from *The Star-Ledger* had recently discovered while researching his story—to give up its crank phones back in the late 1950s. In his article, the reporter had called the town an anachronism, with its square park surrounded by stately Victorian homes, a park with dirt paths crisscrossing to opposite corners. *X* marked the spot. No one in town knew whether to be insulted or pleased by the reference. But they had little time to ponder such trivialities. They were far too worried about what was happening to them.

If the disease had been the only issue, they would have probably shrugged it off. But a few of the more astute citizens, like Clyde Zukowski, the custodian at the high school, and Marge Woodley, who ran the Laundromat on Main Street, and dozens of other concerned residents, had pieced together, from shreds of recent events, a tapestry of terror. Floods of frogs, black clouds of crows, tornadoes of mosquitoes, blistering heat waves followed by blizzards dumping more than a half foot of snow in early spring, killing new buds. It wasn't natural, they said. And most of Bellehaven's citizens had begun to agree.

The same ambitious young reporter who had called the town an anachronism had also stumbled upon the legend of Jessup Wildemere. Seeing the possibilities for an intriguing feature story, maybe something that might be picked up by the Associated Press and published nationwide, he set out to reveal the infamous past of Bellehaven, suggesting it might be the only town in the county, perhaps in the entire state, to have hanged a man the day after he'd been arrested. Maybe that sort of thing happened in the Old West, the reporter wrote, but New Jersey was one of the original thirteen colonies, one of the first states. The law was the very foundation of our new nation. Law-abiding citizens were supposed to lock their alleged criminals in jail until they could be tried before an appointed judge with the benefit of counsel. The reporter had almost gleefully referred to the hanging of Jessup Wildemere as a vigilante brouhaha.

The residents of Bellehaven were in an uproar. They were God-fearing people and Jessup Wildemere was a cold-blooded murderer. Plain and simple. And besides, the incident had taken place more than two hundred years before. It had nothing to do with them.

Still, some people whispered the town had been cursed. A few even believed black magic might be behind the recent chaos. People began to avert their eyes when they passed each other on Main Street or in the aisles of the A&P. Surely someone was to blame for these bizarre events. And it certainly wasn't a man who'd been dead since 1798. For all anyone knew, the source might well be a neighbor, or someone living right under their very own roof. No one knew whom to trust.

They might have tried to explain away the frogs, the crows, and mosquitoes. But this many cases of West Nile virus in one small town had them sick with fear. That was why a team from the National Institutes of Health had recently set up camp in the Riverstone Bed and Breakfast beside the Delaware. That was why nervous news teams made sure to douse themselves with insect repellant before they set foot outside their vans.

People who never turned on the nightly news now sat religiously in front of their TVs every evening at six o'clock, clicking their remotes, hopping back and forth between the major networks, attempting to catch a glimpse of themselves or their neighbors being interviewed. Bellehaven and its West Nile virus "epidemic" were big news on all the stations.

The NIH tried to calm fears by explaining that most people wouldn't get sick from a mosquito carrying the virus. Some might experience flulike symptoms. Only a rare few might become extremely ill. Right now, the mosquito population was minimal. The blizzard had brought them under control. Since the disease showed up five to fifteen days after the person had been bitten, the people from NIH deduced that the residents who were currently suffering from symptoms had probably received bites during the four-day heat wave.

Despite the assurances of public health officials, residents began to panic. People who discovered even a single mosquito bite lined up outside Dr. Braddock's office across the street from the south side of the park, making a line that extended halfway around the block.

The town council held an emergency meeting and voted to begin spraying earlier than usual. For two nights in a row, people were instructed to close windows and to bring pets and lawn furniture indoors while trucks drove through neighborhoods spraying thick clouds of insecticide.

The more fainthearted residents even went so far as to pack up their vans and SUVs with their children, pets, and a few basic necessities and head out of town until the whole thing blew over.

The next morning the headline in the *Bellehaven Press* read "West Nile Virus Claims Its First Bellehaven Victim." The unfortunate casualty was an eighty-seven-year-old man who had lived alone in a small trailer near the river. Devin's hands were shaking as she scanned the article while she stirred a pot of oatmeal for her brothers and sisters. By now the doctors had determined that her grandmother had also been stricken with the virus. They were concerned that it might develop into the sometimes deadly encephalitis.

Like everyone else in town, Devin had begun to think the residents of Bellehaven had been singled out. Cursed for reasons no one understood. With the count of cases rising daily, more people began to leave town. They took their children out of school, apparently not caring one whit whether their kids would have to spend July and August in summer school to make up the work. Some of the McCaffertys' neighbors on Meadowlark Drive had gone to stay with relatives in nearby towns; others had taken rooms in motels outside the county.

As soon as school was out, Devin headed for the bus stop. She was meeting her mother at the hospital. Since she and Kyle had split, Devin didn't dare ask him to give her a ride. And Danny had track.

Kyle was taking their breakup harder than she'd expected. If they passed each other in the hall, he wouldn't look at her. Because they no longer met after fourth period or ate lunch together in the cafeteria, Devin, who had no appetite at all these days, had taken to spending her lunch period in a stall in the girls' room writing in her journal.

She had developed her own code because it was too

risky to write about what had really been happening in her life. If the cops ever confiscated her journal, they wouldn't know what to make of it. Or so she hoped. Sometimes she wrote her sentences backward. Mih ot netsil reve I did yhw? Sometimes she wrote obscure poems that held meaning for her alone. Sometimes she scribbled images in metaphor. *I am at the bottom of a well. The walls are damp and slimy. My fingers slip on the mossy stones. Sometimes I think I will never be able to pull myself out of this dark place.*

The police, if they ever got their hands on her journal, would assume these were the adolescent hormone-induced rages of an overly angst-ridden teen. She was counting on it.

At least she didn't have to worry about memorizing lines for *Macbeth* anymore. The day before, she'd told the drama coach, Mr. Newcombe, about her grandmother's illness and how she would probably have to miss a lot more rehearsals than she already had because she'd be spending a lot of time at the hospital. She had told him she couldn't possibly concentrate on her role.

What she didn't tell Mr. Newcombe was that Lady Macbeth's lines had begun to creep into her thoughts at the most unfortunate times, like on the bus on her way to the hospital. *O, these flaws and starts,/Imposters to true fear, would well become/A woman's story at a winter's fire,/Authorized by her grandam. Shame itself!* You couldn't grab your head, tear at your hair, rub the palm of your hand, and scream, *Out, damned spot! out, I say!* in front of a busful of people, no matter how desperately you wanted to.

Mrs. McCafferty was slumped in the single chair, staring at the wall, a magazine lying open on her lap, when Devin came through the door to her grandmother's room. Since the doctors had determined that Devin's grandmother had West Nile virus, which wasn't contagious, they had moved her into a double room.

A young girl, about Devin's age, was in the other bed, the one by the door. An IV needle was taped to her hand. She appeared to be asleep. And since no one was visiting her, Devin quietly lifted the empty chair from the girl's side of the room and set it next to her mother's. "How is she?" Devin whispered.

"It's progressed to encephalitis." Her mother stared down at the magazine in her lap. "They're making arrangements to move her to the intensive care unit."

Encephalitis. Devin looked over at her sleeping grandmother. The woman's face was ashen. Dried spittle caked the corners of her thin lips. Devin had an overwhelming urge to put her arms around her grandmother and hold on for dear life. Instead she wrapped her fingers around the arms of the chair. "So how are they treating it?"

"Dr. Chu says they've had some success with a drug called Ribavirin."

Devin waited for her mother to go on. When she didn't, Devin said, "So that's what they're giving her?"

Her mother slapped the magazine closed and tossed it on the floor beside the chair. "Yes." Her eyes shifted away from her daughter.

"But . . . ?" Devin saw the unspoken word in her mother's expression.

Mrs. McCafferty sighed. "Your grandmother doesn't seem to be responding to the medication."

"Why not?" Devin's legs had begun to twitch. She locked her ankles around the chair legs.

"They aren't sure. Dr. Chu says this could be a new strain of the virus, one they haven't dealt with before."

"So now what?"

"They're doing what they can—intravenous fluids, nutrition. Mostly they have to be careful she doesn't get some other kind of infection, like pneumonia."

"What about antibiotics?" Devin said. "They can give her those, right?"

"If she gets a bacterial infection, yes. But this is a virus, honey. Antibiotics won't have any effect on it." Her mother got up and walked to the single window. The only view was a brick wall across an air shaft.

"I'll stay here if you want to walk around," Devin said.

Her mother nodded, although her back was still to Devin. "I need to stretch my legs a bit." She reached for her handbag on the table beside the bed. "If Gram wakes up . . ." She paused and looked down at Devin. "If she should say something, well . . . odd, don't get upset, okay?"

Devin blinked back at her. "What's that supposed to mean? Odd?"

Mrs. McCafferty slid the strap of her purse over her shoulder and shrugged. "Encephalitis can cause mental confusion."

"What kind of mental confusion?"

"The doctor called it altered mental states."

"So, has Gram been saying weird things to you or something?"

"She seemed a little agitated earlier today. That's all." Mrs. McCafferty put her arms around Devin and gave her a gentle hug. "I just thought I should warn you."

When her mother was gone, Devin slid the chair closer to the bed. She would spend some time with her grandmother; then, as soon as her mother returned, she would go down to the ICU and see if she could find out how Simon was doing. Liz had told her Tuesday morning in school how she had sneaked in to see Simon the afternoon before, and how she believed one of his fingers had moved. Devin had been hopeful. But then on Wednesday, there had been rumors at school that Simon had taken a turn for the worse on Tuesday afternoon. Devin didn't know whom to believe. So she was determined to see for herself.

She reached through the side rail and touched her grandmother's hand. Her skin felt like fine-grained sandpaper.

She thought about the day her grandparents moved into the already cramped Cape Cod on Meadowlark Drive, how furious she had been with them, with her parents, with the world in general. They had stolen her new bedroom right out from under her. Never mind that Granddad McCafferty was in a wheelchair, unable to talk or move. He was a thief! They both were.

Devin had made sure everyone was at the kitchen table, eating dinner, the night she stomped through the room with the first box, passing them to get to the basement door. All in all, she carried four boxes and two armloads of clothes from her closet to the cellar, and not one member of her family ever looked up from the table or said a word. They just kept right on eating as if Devin's moving into the basement was the most natural thing in the world.

As she sat there holding her grandmother's hand, Devin thought maybe it really *was* the most natural thing, although her intention at the time had been to make them all feel guilty. They had banished her to the basement, after all. A dark hole where you could feel the tickle of tiny feet and tails on your arms as the mice scurried across the bed, where spiders wove webs over your lips while you slept. Or so she sometimes imagined. But no one had forced her to move to the cellar. It had been her own idea.

Now her cozy little corner, curtained away from the rest of them, had become her sanctuary. It wasn't at all what she'd intended. Neither was her grandmother's illness. Still, Devin couldn't help wondering if the silent angry curses she'd heaped on her grandparents each time she passed through the kitchen that night three years before, arms loaded with her few precious belongings, hadn't come back to haunt her.

One of the nurses came in to change the IV bag. She smiled at Devin. "I'm just checking on her," she said as she slipped a clean plastic cover on the thermometer and held it inside Mrs. McCafferty's ear. She checked her pulse and blood pressure, then wrote something on the paper on her clipboard. "They'll be down soon to take her to the ICU," she told Devin as she headed out the door.

When Devin looked back at her grandmother, she was startled to see the old woman's glassy eyes staring up at her. "How are you feeling, Gram?"

Her grandmother didn't answer. She kept her eyes on Devin. Then, as her grandmother's lips slowly parted, Devin had the strangest sensation that time itself had slowed down.

"They know," her grandmother whispered.

Later that night, in her corner of the basement, Devin lay in bed on her side with her pillow curled into her stomach. Not only was her grandmother's illness worse, but the nurses in the ICU had confirmed that Simon's condition was still critical. Devin had come away feeling that he might be even worse than the nurses had let on. It was only an intuition. But it was a strong one.

She pressed her forehead against the cool pillowcase, unable to sleep. She kept thinking about what her grandmother had said, wondering who "they" were. When it came right down to it, probably her grandmother didn't know either. Her warning—or whatever it was—had no doubt been a feverish outburst caused by her illness. That altered mental state Devin's mother had mentioned earlier.

But despite her attempts to reassure herself, Devin's mind kept returning to a story she had seen one night on the national news. Stunned, she had watched as lightning knocked a man right out of his Birkenstocks as he stood at the back of his cabin cruiser in a thunderstorm down in Key West. The man had a can of Coors in his hand, his face turned up to the drenching rain, and was shouting, "Okay, let's see your best shot. I dare you!" And of course, "they" took him up on it. With one swift bolt of lightning, the guy was history. The video had been filmed by one of the deceased man's friends, who had been standing in the cabin doorway at the time.

Devin's father had been watching the news with her. He leaned forward in his recliner, slapped his knee, and held his palm out to the TV. "Well, what the hell did he think was going to happen? You stand out there in the middle of the ocean during an electrical storm, you're going to end up toast!"

But Devin couldn't help feeling there was more to it than the scientific inevitability her father's explanation implied. For some reason, she had thought of the ancient Greek plays she had studied in her English class, and of the Furies. Those ministers of punishment. Those emissaries of swift justice. It didn't matter who or what "they" were—the gods, the fates, supernatural forces—you simply did not mock them. *Ever.*

Wasn't that what she'd been doing for the past three years, she and Kyle and the others, thumbing their noses at "them"? Outright daring "them" to do something about it? She rolled onto her back but kept a tight hold on the pillow, pressing it against her chest as if it could cushion any blows that might come her way.

Simon was sitting on Mr. Neidermeyer's split-rail fence with Jessup Wildemere when it occurred to him that he had never seen Jessup move beyond the area canopied by the branches of the Liberty Tree. It was as if Jessup was being held captive, locked in by some invisible force field.

When Simon asked Jessup where he lived, knowing full well he was treading on touchy ground, since Jessup wasn't actually *living* at all, Jessup gave him a blank look. He didn't seem to grasp the situation. Not in the same way Simon did.

Jessup said, "I have been wondering the same about you." It wasn't an answer and Simon was disappointed.

"It's like I said before, I'm from here." This time he didn't mention Bellehaven.

It was barely dawn. Dark clouds hid the sun. A steady, soft rain was falling, but there wasn't so much as a spot of water on Jessup. His clothes were as dry as dust. Simon, too, remained bone-dry.

Jessup slid off the fence and began to pace, slow steps that took him only to the very tips of the longest branches and back again. "I know everyone in these parts. The name Gray is not familiar."

"Who is it you keep waiting for?" Simon asked, hoping to change the subject. "Every time I come to this place, you're here waiting."

Jessup rubbed his fingers across his forehead, looking puzzled. "Yes. That's true. It has been a long wait."

"How long?"

Jessup looked over at Simon; his expression shifted from blank to bewildered. "I don't know. I can't seem to recall when I first came here."

Simon's skin rippled with goose bumps. He had suddenly realized that he, too, had begun to lose count of how many times he had come here. It seemed he was spending more and more time with Jessup and less in the hospital. But he couldn't say for certain how much time had passed. He no longer traveled the halls of the intensive care unit, no longer visited Stanley Isaacson, or found himself in his bedroom at home, or down by the river. The only place he came to was the Liberty Tree. And he had no idea why that should be. He knew there must be some connection, but he still had no recollection of the accident and no idea why he was in the hospital.

"Are you here to meet someone again?" Simon was hoping Jessup's answer would help him solve his own mystery. Maybe he was supposed to meet someone too.

"Hannah." Jessup stared over at the Gulf station. But Simon knew from what Jessup had told him before that he saw only a narrow dirt road leading to the green at the center of what, in 1798, could scarcely be called a town.

"Hannah?"

Jessup looked worried. "You must swear not to say a word to anyone."

"About what?"

"Hannah Dobbler."

"Why not?"

Jessup frowned at Simon. "I shouldn't be meeting her here at all. She is betrothed to Elias Belcher." He cocked his head to one side and narrowed his eyes. "If you are truly from around here, you would know that."

Simon ignored Jessup's observation. "Why are you meeting her, then?" But Simon thought he already knew the answer to that. He'd been living a similar story for the past year.

"She doesn't love Elias Belcher," Jessup said. "He is widowed with five children and has barely a tooth left in his mouth."

"Then why would she marry him?"

"Her father has arranged the marriage. Cornelius Dobbler's land borders Elias's. They are old friends. And their two properties together will amount to several thousand acres."

Simon was only now beginning to realize that Hannah Dobbler was the daughter of the man Jessup Wildemere had murdered.

The rain had stopped, but a heavy fog had crept over the area. Jessup Wildemere blurred in the mist. Simon jumped down from the fence. He knew what was going to happen, knew Jessup was going to kill Cornelius Dobbler. Simon had to stop him. He reached out, but his hand found only air.

He wanted to know what had happened to Hannah. Why hadn't she come? He wanted to know if Jessup would get a chance to see her one last time.

The fog was so thick he could no longer see the Liberty Tree. No matter which way he turned, he found only the damp gray mist.

Chapter 11

ANOTHER HEAT WAVE HAD MOVED INTO BELLEHAVEN, sending ripples of alarm and fear up and down the streets. People worried that the mosquitoes might start to hatch again if the weather didn't turn cooler soon, which could mean more cases of West Nile virus. Fifteen more families packed up and left town.

Late Thursday night, Liz sat on the floor of her bedroom in shorts and a T-shirt, her back against the foot of the bed, with both bedroom windows wide open, her notebook in her lap, and Pandora stretched out against her leg. Pandora's chin and one paw rested on Liz's thigh. Liz was on her third cup of coffee and fourth Snickers bar, and it was only eleven-thirty. Already her handwriting had the jagged, frazzled look of a caffeine-sugar high. But if she was ever going to get her paper done for Mrs. Rosen by the next day, it would mean pulling an all-nighter.

It was her own fault, of course. Liz had found Lucinda Alderman's diary almost a week earlier, sneaked it home in her backpack, glanced at the first few incredibly boring pages, and hadn't bothered to look at it since. She had other things on her mind. Namely Simon. Lately she'd been spending every afternoon and early evening at the hospital, sitting in the waiting room outside the ICU, hoping for some word.

Courtney wasn't at all informative. When she returned to the waiting room between her ten-minute visits, she slumped into a chair, eyes closed, and listened to whatever was on her Discman. The music was turned up so loud Liz could hear it even though Courtney wore earphones.

Mr. Gray at least nodded to Liz, or mumbled some form of greeting, although he never sat in the waiting room with Courtney, as far as Liz could tell. Still, she continued to show up every day, hoping she hadn't misread the signs—that almost indiscernible feather-light movement of Simon's finger—hoping that each minute, each hour, he was struggling to come back to them. But every evening Liz left the hospital disappointed.

She had barely been able to keep up with her regular homework assignments. Spending extra hours researching her history project was more than she could handle. Earlier in the marking period, before her enthusiasm for the assignment had dwindled to almost zero, she had managed to pull together a fairly decent account of daily life in 1798 Bellehaven, or Havenhill, as the town was called back then.

At the historical society she had even discovered an old map from 1787, the year New Jersey became a state. The park was the green in those days, the heart of the town, as in many ways it still was. Only a few homes and shops were scattered around the green, and only one main road came into town. On the outskirts were a number of farms. The one closest to the green, as far as she'd been able to find out, was the Alderman farm. The boundary of the Dobbler farm, one of the largest in the area, abutted the Alderman farm on one side, and another farm, owned by Elias Belcher, on the other. The town's population, according to census records from that time, was 107.

Old court records turned up even less information, a single entry for September third "on which day, in the year of our Lord 1798, the execution of one Jessup Wildemere for the brutal murder of Cornelius Dobbler was carried out." When Liz first stumbled upon this information, a few days before she found the Alderman journal, she had realized almost at once the discrepancy in the date. Local legend had the people of Havenhill hanging Jessup Wildemere in the dead of winter, after a severe blizzard and a dangerous food shortage. The court records, however, stated that the execution took place in late summer.

Liz had been so excited by this unexpected find that she'd spent the following Saturday gravitating back and forth between the county library and the historical society looking for other errors in the account of the execution. But so far that was all she had to go on. That, and Lucinda Alderman's journal, which she had yet to finish reading.

Somehow she couldn't imagine Mrs. Rosen being impressed by something so insignificant as a discrepancy in a date. Still, if that much was questionable, Liz wondered, what other facts might have gotten changed or distorted over thousands of verbal retellings?

Liz ran her fingers through Pandora's soft fur as she swallowed the last of her coffee. Given the sticky weather, iced tea would have made more sense. But she was afraid tea wouldn't pack enough of a caffeine jolt to keep her awake. The heat in the room didn't help. It made her drowsy.

She got up, pulled the oscillating fan from her closet, set it on the desk near the window, and plugged it in. For a few minutes she stood in front of the fan, letting the cool air chill her sweating skin. Then she reached for her backpack and pulled out Lucinda Alderman's journal.

She flopped on her bed, stomach down, and had begun to flip through the pages when a sudden motion caught her attention. Across the room a large black feather danced recklessly in front of the fan, finally coming to rest on the page of her open book. Liz stared at the feather, then glanced up at the window. The screen was down. She looked at the sleeping Pandora.

Pandora opened one eye, stretched, and rested her chin on her paws. If she was the guilty party, she didn't look the least bit contrite. But it was unlikely the cat would have gone after any of the crows. Liz had watched her hide under the front porch whenever the birds took over the trees in her yard. They were, after all, as big as Pandora.

Liz blew the feather from the page and went back to looking for entries made in 1798. Unfortunately, Lucinda wasn't consistent with her entries. Some had dates, others did not. As she read through the pages Liz discovered that Lucinda was the wife of a farmer, Joseph Alderman, and the mother of their four children. From what Liz could tell, the woman was not much older than twenty-five at the time she began the journal.

In between sipping two more cups of coffee and scarfing down half a bag of Hershey's Kisses, Liz skimmed through boring accounts of Lucinda's daily chores, household records, and descriptions of her children's antics. About a third of the way through the journal, when Liz was just about to pack it in and begin writing her paper on the only discrepancy she had—the date of the execution—she stumbled upon Jessup Wildemere's name.

> *My husband, Joseph, has brought home a most comely and well educated young man who goes by the name of Jessup Wildemere, and who hails from New York. He tells us his father's estate is on the Hudson and that he is going to Philadelphia to seek his fortune. My Joseph has enlisted the young man's help this spring. We have welcomed Master Jessup into our home as he is in need of employment if he is to continue his journey south.*

Liz stared at the page. Comely? Well educated? Young? This was not at all how she had imagined Jessup Wildemere, the filthy, murderous drifter of legend. Surely there was a mix-up somewhere. Surely Lucinda Alderman wasn't talking about the same man?

Pandora hopped on the bed and curled into a furry ball on Liz's back. Liz glanced at the clock on her nightstand. It was two in the morning. Maybe she was hallucinating? Maybe she was half asleep and dreaming. She rolled over—sending Pandora sliding—and looked up at the ceiling light. The glare hurt her eyes. No, she was definitely awake.

Liz's heart had begun to race, and not just from the sugar and caffeine. She couldn't believe her luck. Just when she had all but given up, here it was, the very thing she had been searching for. Lucinda Alderman's account showed more than just a little discrepancy in the character of Jessup Wildemere as he appeared in local stories.

No matter how long it took her to wade through Lucinda's tedious prose and barely legible handwriting, Liz was determined to stick with it. Somewhere in this long-forgotten piece of domestic scribbling there had to be some mention of Cornelius Dobbler's murder and the subsequent execution of Jessup Wildemere. Liz was counting on it.

The call came just before dawn on Friday. Devin heard the phone but rolled over to face the basement wall. Her mother would answer it. There was a phone by her parents' bed. Still, Devin found herself listening for her mother's footsteps overhead. In her heart she knew this call was about her grandmother.

The basement door squeaked open. The light came on and Devin heard someone coming down the steps. A moment later her mother's shadow stretched across the room. She gave Devin a gentle shake and signaled her to follow.

They stood in the middle of the kitchen, Devin in a T-shirt and bikini briefs, her mother in a summer nightgown with tiny yellow roses. They kept their voices low so as not to wake the others.

"That was the hospital," her mother said. She reached over to brush Devin's tangled hair away from her face. "I need you to watch the kids. You can call Mrs. Needham after seven and ask if she'd mind coming over to stay with your granddad so the rest of you can go to school. And ask her if she'd mind taking care of the kids when they get home this afternoon." Mrs. Needham, a retired beautician who lived across the street with her eldest son, Vincent, sometimes baby-sat for the McCaffertys in emergencies. Devin had a sinking feeling that this was going to be one of those emergencies.

She began to shiver. She felt cold all over, although it was suffocatingly warm in the small house. How could her mother even think of sending her to school when Gram was so sick? "What did they say? Is she going to be okay?"

"She's in a coma. Dr. Chu said Gram had a number of small seizures last night shortly before it happened."

"Dad . . . ," Devin said, her voice trailing off like a

stifled sob. Darrell McCafferty was on the road, hauling a truckload of hair spray, cartons and cartons of it, to a distribution center in Newark. Devin squinted at the clock on the stove. Right about now her father was probably sleeping at a rest stop somewhere on I-80 outside of Chicago.

"I know," her mother said.

She knew her mother was thinking the same thing. Her father's mother might be dying, and he was on the road somewhere. At the moment he had no idea of what was going on back in Bellehaven. "I want to go with you," she told her mother.

"Devin, I need you to be here right now. There's no one else to watch the kids and Granddad. I don't want to call Mrs. Needham this early." She could hear the unspoken "I'm sorry" in her mother's voice.

"What if she's dying, Mom?" Tears trembled on Devin's eyelashes. "I want to be there with her."

Mrs. McCafferty circled her arms around her daughter. "Honey, your gram's one tough lady. She's not going to give up without a fight." She leaned back and smiled. "And neither are we."

Devin showed up at the hospital less than a half hour after Mrs. Needham arrived. If her mother was angry about her cutting school, she never said a word. She only nodded, then left Devin alone with her grandmother for her ten-minute visit while she went down to the cafeteria for coffee.

Standing beside her grandmother's bed, watching the

lines blip across the monitor, Devin thought of Simon, a few doors down. Her grandmother was still able to breathe on her own and so, unlike Simon, didn't have a respirator. But the curtain was drawn over the window and another curtain covered the glass wall, shutting out the glare of the fluorescent lights in the main room of the ICU, just as they did in Simon's room. One of the nurses had explained to her that the purpose of keeping the room dim was so the light wouldn't damage her grandmother's eyes if she suddenly came out of the coma after a long period.

When Devin's ten minutes were up, she left her grandmother's room and, since no one was watching her, slipped into Simon's. He was still pale, but the swelling in his lips had gone down. The fading bruises had a faint yellowish cast.

She took his limp hand in hers. She wondered if people in comas were in an actual place, a kind of limbo in a different dimension. Maybe it was childish, but she liked to think her grandmother and Simon were together, and that maybe they would help each other find their way back.

Anyone walking down Main Street in Bellehaven late that afternoon would have thought they had stumbled upon a ghost town. Not a single person ventured onto the streets. All was still, except for a few scraps of discarded paper and dead leaves, caught in a playful breeze, shuffling back and forth over sidewalks sticky with bird droppings from the crows. A few of the shops along Main Street sported Closed signs on their doors, although with several news crews and the team from NIH in town, most of the merchants were willing to keep their stores open, West Nile virus or no West Nile virus.

This was how Main Street appeared when Devin, on her way back to town from the bus stop, decided to pass right by the turnoff that led to her street and keep on going. She was acutely aware of the sound of her footsteps as she walked past the shops, past Chrissie's Deli, Garden Creations, Flynn's Liquors, and the Auto Spa, and past the scattered antiques and craft shops with names like The Country Goose, where her mother worked part-time. She crossed at the only intersection in town that had a traffic light, although no cars were in sight, and kept on going until the shops became a few small houses, their front porches only inches from the sidewalk. Ahead was the bridge that connected New Jersey and Pennsylvania.

When she was almost to the guardhouse by the bridge, she changed course and headed down a dirt road. A heavy metal chain stretched across the entrance to the road. A sign warned No Trespassing. But Devin knew this was the quickest way to get down to the river, and that was where she was headed.

Her mother had decided to stay on at the hospital until visiting hours were over, even though she could only visit her mother-in-law for ten minutes each hour. Devin knew she should go straight home and help Mrs. Needham cook dinner for the kids, knew she was being horribly selfish. But so much weighed on her right now, and she had a splitting headache. The pressure pounded on the inside of her skull. The thought of being trapped in a house full of screaming kids was worse than some medieval torture. She needed to be alone.

For the next hour she sat on a large flat rock by the river's edge, eyes closed, listening to the sounds of the birds. Every so often she opened her eyes and shaded them with her hand to watch goldfinches dart overhead at top speed, somehow navigating their way through a complex tangle of tree branches while still in flight. Even the most skilled pilot could never achieve such a feat.

Watching the birds helped to calm her. They also made her think of Simon—the time the two of them had returned from the mall where Simon had helped her pick out a CD for Kyle's birthday. It had been early evening and they'd parked her mother's car by the boat ramp so they could walk along the river. Something she and Kyle never did. A simple walk would have been far too passive an activity for Kyle, who preferred more challenging undertakings, productive endeavors that would score points with college admissions directors. Anything else was a waste of time.

She and Simon had come to this place, this same rock, just in time to watch the sun begin its descent behind the trees. Less than fifty feet away stood an old black birch, its uppermost branches bare and dying. The rest of the tree still had its leaves. As the two of them watched, a flock of goldfinches landed on the bare branches. The birds spread their wings to catch the sunlight. Their bodies flickered bright yellow, like enormous fireflies, as they lifted a few feet off the branches, then settled back down. When the sun touched the top of the tree, right before it sank into the woods, the tree looked as if it were ablaze with a crown of gold.

Sitting side by side, neither of them spoke or took their eyes from the tree, but Devin felt as if all the shimmering light from the tree had somehow transferred itself to her body.

Now, as she stared up at the evening sky, she wasn't in the least surprised to see that it was black with crows. They settled on the branches, leaving no room for the more timid birds. She wished the goldfinches would light up the birch tree again. But that wasn't going to happen. Some things weren't meant to happen twice. At least not in the same way.

But what about people? They sometimes got second chances, didn't they? She had no idea why she was thinking this, except that it seemed important that Simon and her grandmother have a second chance. And maybe she wanted one for herself, too, although she scarcely dared to hope.

How did you manage that—a second chance? Did you bargain with the gods, with the supernatural forces? Make deals with the Furies? With . . . *them*? Because Devin suddenly realized she was willing to do just that—strike a bargain. She wanted to set things right again. She wanted Simon and her grandmother to have a second chance.

She was so lost in thought, she did not notice it had

begun to snow black feathers until she glanced down and saw that a small puddle of them had formed in her lap. She sighed and glared up at the crows.

She got to her feet, brushed the feathers from her clothes, and picked them out of her hair. Then, before she left, she made a deal. She shouted up to the crows that they could darn well make themselves useful and take a message back to "them," tell "them" she would trade her future at Cornell, or any of the schools where she had been accepted under false pretenses, for the lives of Simon and her grandmother. The crows fell silent. Devin had the eerie feeling they were actually listening. One of them lifted off a branch and flew toward the sunset.

Devin's laugh began as a timid giggle, then swelled to a deep gut-bursting belly laugh. She felt lighter than she'd ever imagined possible, so light she had to look down to make sure she was still wearing shoes. She brushed a few feathers from her shoulders, then headed back up the slope toward town.

When she came through the back door a short time later, Devin found Mrs. Needham spooning out canned ravioli for Devin's six siblings. Mrs. Needham was wearing Mr. McCafferty's barbecue apron. Her gray hair was perfectly coifed and her fingernails manicured to within an inch of their lives. After forty-five years as a beautician you didn't exactly go to seed overnight.

Mrs. Needham looked up as Devin came through the door. She let the empty pan drop in the sink with a clatter and frowned at Devin as if to say, You're too late.

Devin felt guilty about leaving Mrs. Needham holding the bag. "I'll take care of the dishes when everyone's done," she said as she headed down the hall to her room.

The first thing she did was to sit down at her desk and begin to compose letters of regret to Cornell, Middlebury, and Lafayette. Monday she would take the bus to the community college and pick up an application. And in between she would go right on praying there was still time to undo what she had done.

Roger Garvey poured himself a cup of coffee and sat on the corner of Debra Santino's desk, grinning. The lieutenant couldn't for the life of her figure out what he was so happy about. They still didn't have any solid leads on the breach of security at Bellehaven High. Not one of Simon's friends had revealed a single incriminating piece of evidence during her interrogation on Tuesday, although it hadn't escaped her attention that Devin McCafferty had grown increasingly agitated and defensive before the interview was over. It could be she was hiding something. Debra planned to follow up on that, perhaps come at the girl with a different line of questioning.

Roger was rapping his knuckles on her desk. It was nine o'clock on a Friday night and they were still at work. She'd already called home and told Steve to order pizza for him and the girls and to save a few slices for her. Roger, she knew, had a hot date. He'd been talking about it all week. So he was the last person she expected to see sitting on her desk, looking as if he'd just won the state lottery.

"You want to hear a funny story?" he asked.

Debra figured, what the heck, it had been a long day. She could use a good laugh. "Sure."

"It looks like that computer teacher, George McCabe, has been visiting porn sites on the school's time."

Caught off guard, the lieutenant let out a throaty "Ha!" She shook her head in disbelief. "You're kidding! So . . . what? You think he's filling in his free period with a little entertainment instead of grading papers?"

Roger ran his hand through his dark, neatly trimmed hair and took a swallow of lukewarm coffee. He had deep dimples that made him look boyish. "Actually, I think it's more complicated than that."

"Really?" Debra wondered what else Roger had found on the data they had downloaded from the school server two weeks earlier.

"Yeah. I sort of doubt he was able to log on to several sites at one time. I mean, he could, using several computers in the school lab. But what would be the point?"

Debra shifted her gaze away from Roger and stared across the room, thinking. "So you're saying whoever got hold of his password was using it for more than academic gain?"

Roger was grinning again. "Okay, here's the thing," he said. "I don't know if we're talking about the same kids you've been questioning. We could be. Or maybe there's more than one group involved."

Debra rubbed her forehead as if she had a pounding headache. "You've lost me."

"The log from the server shows McCabe, or someone, was tied in to multiple sites, all porn sites, at the same time. Multiple sites show up dozens of times under his account. It looks like six, seven, sometimes even more people, were accessing different sites all at the same time, and almost always between three and five in the afternoon." He paused and waited for the lieutenant's reaction.

She stared back at him, frowning.

"I think maybe McCabe was letting them do it," he said finally.

"You mean he *gave* some of the students his password?"

"You got it."

"But why?"

"Who knows? No wonder the man was sweating bullets when we were downloading all this stuff. I figured it was the heat wave, but it looks like he had other reasons." Roger got up from the desk and headed over to the coffeepot for a refill. "I figured you might want to talk to McCabe before we go any further with this."

Debra leaned back in her chair. She looked thoughtful. "Interesting."

"What?"

"Barbara Schroder was the one who wanted to bring us in on the case. George McCabe didn't seem to know much about it. And yet he's the one person who's really in a position to know. You'd think he'd be the first one to figure out something was going on and blow the whistle on whoever was getting into the system."

"He probably kept quiet because he had a few things going on himself," Roger said.

Debra shook her head. "I thought the school had software to filter out those porn sites, Cyber Patrol or something."

"They do. But McCabe maintains the network, remember? He could easily have set up an account to bypass any firewalls."

"So do you think it was Simon Gray who was checking out these porn sites?"

Roger shrugged. "I have no idea who's involved. But like I said, there's more than one person. Simon Gray could be one of them."

"This doesn't sound like the kids I've been questioning. All of them are involved in after-school activities. Legit activities," she added when she saw Roger's grin.

"Well, McCabe *did* tell us Simon Gray was his best student—a real computer whiz."

"You know, given this latest information, it's a little suspicious that McCabe told us what he did." Debra frowned. "It's as if he wanted us to check out Gray."

"Well, sure he did. He knew what the kid was capable of."

"Okay. But why do you suppose McCabe gave us Simon Gray's name as a possible suspect and no one else's? Now you're saying there's more than one kid involved. Do you think McCabe did it to throw us off the track?"

"Who knows? But I wouldn't rule out Gray just yet."

"I wasn't planning to. It was just a thought." She glanced down at her wristwatch. "You're a little late for that date, aren't you?"

"I already called her. She said no problem. She's fixing a late dinner for the two of us." He grinned, downed the last of his coffee, and headed for the door. "I'd still follow up with McCabe. Just a suggestion. You never know where it might lead."

But Debra Santino was already one step ahead of him. The minute he was out the door she called Barbara Schroder at home and arranged to meet with her and George McCabe at the school first thing Saturday morning, weekend or no weekend.

Chapter 12

Saturday night Kyle was stuck at home. He had a paper on Thomas Hardy's *Jude the Obscure* due for AP English on Monday and hadn't even begun to write it. If he didn't get an A on the paper, he could jeopardize his A average in the course.

Ordinarily he would have had the paper done before the weekend, but his concentration was all screwed up. He couldn't get Devin out of his mind. He was angry as hell at her. Angry at her for messing up their last two months of school, for screwing up their plans for the prom and prom weekend at the shore. Why would she break up with him before school was out? It didn't make sense. Not that he hadn't been planning to break it off himself before he left for Harvard. He figured they'd probably both want to be free to see other people once they got to college. But that was months away. They could be having the time of their lives right now. It was their senior year, for god's sake. He couldn't believe she'd done this to him after all the years they'd been together. And the worst part was, he still didn't have a clue what was behind it.

He might have sat at his desk, staring at the blank page on his monitor, all night, if his mother hadn't suddenly showed up at his bedroom door to announce that Danny was waiting outside for him.

He found Danny parked by the front curb in his Mustang. Kyle leaned his arms on the roof of the car and peered inside the open window on the passenger side. "What's up?"

Danny stared at Kyle as if he hadn't heard him right. "Hendershot's party, man. Remember?"

"Yeah, right. I forgot. I've been working on that Hardy paper." Kyle jerked his thumb toward the house.

"Get in," Danny said. "We'll pick up Devin."

Kyle looked away and didn't say anything.

"Or not," Danny added.

"She's probably at the hospital," Kyle told him. He'd been dodging Danny's questions about Devin and him since Wednesday. But he could tell Danny wasn't buying it.

Danny shrugged and looked down at the steering wheel. "So . . . is it off between you guys?"

"Like I said, man, she's been at the hospital a lot." Kyle drummed his thumbs on the roof of the car. "That's all. Her grandmother's sick. Jeez, give her a break."

"Maybe she'll be at Hendershot's party," Danny said.

Kyle doubted Devin would be at the party, although there was a small chance she'd show up with a few of her friends. In truth, he hoped she wouldn't be there, because then it would be obvious to everyone they weren't together anymore. And he wasn't in the mood to spend the night doling out explanations.

"So are you coming or not?" Danny said.

Kyle thought for a moment about the paper on Hardy, decided he would spend all day Sunday on it, and climbed into the front seat. Devin or no Devin, he had little more than two months left of his senior year, and he was determined to make the most of them.

The sounds of heavy metal reverberated through the night air. Danny could feel the bass as soon as they turned onto Trip Hendershot's street. Cars lined both sides of the block. The Hendershots' front yard had been converted into a parking lot. Danny didn't want to park on the lawn, where the cars were wedged so tight it was almost impossible to get the doors open. He wasn't about to risk getting his 'Stang messed up. Instead, he dropped Kyle off and drove two blocks away to park by a deserted curb. He made sure the car was out in the open, not parked beneath any crow-laden trees.

When he got to the Hendershots', he found Kyle standing in the breakfast nook, watching a bunch of kids toss Ping-Pong balls into large Styrofoam cups of beer.

"She here?" Danny asked. They both knew he was talking about Devin.

Kyle shook his head and opened a can of Coke. Danny helped himself to a beer from one of the three ice-filled coolers on the floor by the back door.

"You want me to drive you over to her house?"

A roar of laughter echoed from the group surrounding the table after Trip Hendershot's Ping-Pong ball missed the cups of beer by a mile. Someone handed him one of the full cups and he chugged it, losing half the contents down the front of his T-shirt.

When Kyle didn't bother to answer, Danny shrugged and wandered downstairs to the family room. He was pretty sure something had happened between Kyle and Devin, but it wasn't any of his business. Better to stay out of it.

On one side of the family room, a few jocks from the football team were watching Trip Hendershot's videotape of November's homecoming game. The big-screen TV provided the only light in the room. Some of the kids were dancing, although you could hardly hear the music above the football video. Others were making out on the huge U-shaped sectional couch at the other end of the room.

Danny was about to go back upstairs when Alan Caldwell, a senior who played tight end for the Bellehaven Bobcats, came leaping down the stairs, almost knocking Danny off his feet. He tapped two of the other players on the shoulder and signaled them to follow.

There was something about the expression on Alan Caldwell's face that made Danny curious. He trailed after the three guys, staying at a reasonable distance. They headed outside to the deck. Danny could see them through the kitchen window above the sink. He didn't want to be obvious. If he went out on the deck, they would probably stop talking about whatever it was that was going on. Instead, he hoisted himself onto the kitchen counter beside the sink and leaned his head back against the wall. His left ear was only inches from the open window. With the music blasting through the house, it was difficult to hear, but he was able to catch a few words. And the more he listened, the faster his heart beat. Because what he heard Alan Caldwell tell the others was "The game's up."

Ten minutes later Danny had brought Kyle to the wooded area at the far end of the Hendershots' backyard.

"This better be good," Kyle told him.

"It's good. It's good," Danny reassured him. He kept punching his fist into the palm of his other hand, barely able to contain himself.

Kyle leaned back against a tree and folded his arms across his chest. "So let's hear it."

"I just overheard Alan Caldwell telling Joey Campanelli and Scott Turso he got a call from Mr. McCabe right before he left for the party." The grin widened on Danny's face. "He said the cops met with McCabe and Principal Schroder this morning. They figured out someone's been using the school computers to download porn. Caldwell said McCabe caved, told the cops everything. Whatever that means."

Kyle stared at Danny, his face expressionless. It was obvious he didn't get the connection. "What's this got to do with us?"

Danny snickered. "Man, don't you get it? Caldwell and

some of the other seniors on the football team have been using the school computers to access porn. That means they either hacked into the system, stole McCabe's password, or McCabe let them use it, which would really be stupid. But, hey, you never know." He shrugged. "Somehow they bypassed the firewall."

Kyle studied Danny with interest. "So if there are other students who've either been hacking into the system or have access to McCabe's password, then they could have been downloading other stuff."

"Like exams," Danny said, nodding and laughing at the same time. His laughter bubbled out like hiccups.

Kyle stared at him, trying to take in this interesting twist of fate. Then he laughed even more loudly than Danny.

"This calls for major celebrating," Danny told him. "Let's par-*tay*! I'm getting me a couple of brews. One for each hand."

Kyle grabbed him by the arm as Danny started back to the Hendershots' house. "Not a word. Got it? It sounds to me like the cops think they've got their suspects. So keep your trap shut."

Danny's face sagged. "Have I ever once, in the past three years, ever told anybody about the project? *Ever?*" He jerked his arm from Kyle's grip. "Lighten up, man."

Kyle cocked his head to one side. "We're not out of the woods yet, you know."

"We're not?"

"If the cops found out about the porn sites, who knows what else they'll find?"

Danny's shoulders slumped. He nodded. Kyle was right. They couldn't afford to let their guard down.

But in spite of Kyle's caution, Danny was able to take a full breath for the first time in two weeks. He felt as if he'd gotten his life back. He looked up through the branches of the trees, thick with buds waiting to burst into leaves, and to the sky beyond, ignoring the crows. It was almost impossible to see the stars for all the ground light. Even the North Star wasn't visible tonight. But he knew it was up there, just as sure as he saw his future stretching out before him, huge and glorious.

Jessup Wildemere's clothes were soaked in blood. He stared at Simon as if he'd never seen him before. Simon saw the panic in the man's dark eyes.

"I tried to stop her," Jessup told him, between breaths. Simon could see he had been running hard.

"Who?"

Jessup didn't answer. He bent over, balancing his hands on his knees. "She was like a madwoman." He moaned softly and shook his head as if trying to dislodge the image. "So much blood."

Simon stared at the blood-soaked figure before him as he struggled to remember how the story went. Cornelius Dobbler had been stabbed more than fifty times as he slept in his own bed. There had been so much blood, even the sheets couldn't soak it all up. It had dripped into a pool on the floor, run into the interstices of the loose floorboards, and formed a stain on the parlor ceiling below.

The Dobbler house still stood on Prescott Street. And to this day, not one single family—and there had been seven over the years—residing in the Dobbler house had been able to get rid of the stain, not with sealers, undercoats, sanding, or replastering.

According to the story, a group of men from town had gone out looking for Jessup Wildemere. When they found him, clothes drenched in blood, there wasn't one among them to question his guilt. They simply hauled him off to jail, where he would wait to be tried the next day.

Simon looked over at Jessup, who stared down at his bloodstained hands, then rested his forehead against the coarse bark of the Liberty Tree, eyes closed, as if to shut out some terrible sight. His hands, pressed against the tree, left bloody fingerprints.

Simon thought he heard him whispering Hannah's name. A chilling thought came to him. "Was Hannah there?" Simon asked Jessup.

"Her father discovered us by the riverbank. He was going to force her to marry Elias Belcher this Sunday." Jessup turned to face Simon, who was stunned to see tears in the man's eyes. "Hannah told me not to worry. She would talk some sense into her father. I waited for her tonight. Behind the barn. When she came to me, she still carried the knife. Her clothes were drenched with blood."

"*Hannah* killed her father?" Simon could hardly get his mind around this distortion. This was *not* how the story went.

"I held her, there behind the barn, while she cried." He stared down at his clothes. "Her father's blood is on me as well. As it should be. The crime belongs to us both. I am as guilty as she."

Simon shook his head vehemently. He wanted to tell Jessup that Hannah was the murderer, that he was innocent. But the words wouldn't come.

The hairs on the back of his neck prickled. Simon knew what was going to happen next. The townspeople would come for Jessup. They would put him in jail. Then they would hang him. But the hanging happened in the winter, didn't it? At least that was how Simon remembered the story, although he was beginning to realize there might be considerable flaws in that original tale, the one he'd grown up with.

Jessup looked off into the woods. "She's going to meet me here."

Simon wondered why Hannah hadn't left with Jessup right after she'd met him behind the barn. A horrible thought came to him. Hannah was the only one who knew where Jessup was. Was it Hannah who told the men where to find him?

Simon felt sick. He knew how all this was going to turn out. "You have to leave," he told Jessup.

"Leave Hannah?" Jessup shook his head, as if this wasn't even in the realm of possibility.

"If you wait here for her, they'll find you."

He wanted to shout right in Jessup Wildemere's face that if he didn't get his ass out of there *fast* he was a dead man. That was crazy. Jessup was already dead. He had been for more than two hundred years. And there wasn't a thing Simon or anyone else could do to change that.

Simon was frantic to leave this place. He couldn't bear the thought of Jessup throwing his life away. He covered his eyes, as if he could make the nightmare disappear. When he dared to take his hands away, Simon found himself standing in his own backyard, at the edge of the field.

Overhead the moon was so full and bright, it hurt his eyes. In the cemetery beyond, on the opposite side of the field, stood a woman. Simon knew, as you can only know such things in dreams, that this was his mother. She raised her hand and waved to him.

He looked down at his bare feet, sunk in soft grass, only inches from the edge of the field. He couldn't seem to move beyond this spot. When he looked up again, his mother was gone. A deep, painful loneliness threatened to swallow him whole, from the inside out.

A thick fog began to form. The gravestones seemed to melt into it as it drifted toward him.

All his senses were deadened. He felt nothing. Saw nothing. Tasted nothing. Smelled nothing. Heard nothing. When he tried to breathe, a heaviness pressed down on his chest. He could no longer draw air into his lungs. A terrifying thought seized him. He was dying. This time he would not be returning to the hospital.

From somewhere in the fog he heard a voice. Muffled. Someone was calling his name. The sound was barely a whisper. But he turned his head toward it and listened.

Liz Shapiro dreamed she was digging in the mud with Simon in the backyard of her house. They were once again five years old, and the two of them were smeared from head to toe in cool, delightful ooze. It squished through their fingers and toes as they danced in their soppy underwear beneath raindrops so large they could fill a whole pitcher in less than a minute. But then the rain began to come down in torrents.

As the muddy water rose from the stream in her backyard, Liz ran for the porch, and when she looked over her shoulder she saw that the stream had swelled to the size of the Delaware. It pulled Simon along so fast, she didn't think she would ever be able to reach him. His head bobbed up and down like a rubber ball as he paddled furiously to stay in place.

By now the water had risen to the top step of the porch. Simon's alarmed cries echoed in her head. He was no longer five years old. He was seventeen again. His face was bruised and his head, bandaged. The bandages were brown with muddy water. In a panic Liz looked around for something she could throw to him, something he could grab on to to keep afloat. Simon's cries became more piercing.

Frantic, Liz began to throw the porch furniture into the raging river. Wicker chairs, cushions and all. Anything that might float, anything for him to hold on to. Up ahead was an enormous oak. She had never seen a tree this large, except for pictures of giant redwoods, and certainly never an oak. The river water beat against its lower branches. If Simon could seize one of the branches, maybe he could pull himself out. She shouted to him, screamed for him to grab hold. Simon's voice echoed back to her. He was coming closer to the tree but didn't seem to notice the branches.

"The branches, Simon. Grab one of the branches," Liz yelled.

Simon's cries became the barking caws of crows outside her window. They grew so loud they punctured Liz's dream, like a pin popping a balloon.

She bolted upright and blinked into the glare of moonlight streaking across her bed. Something was wrong. Horribly wrong. She threw the covers back and grabbed a pair of jeans and a T-shirt from the floor. She scribbled a note to her mother, left it on the kitchen table, and snapped up the car keys.

The stars were still out when Liz pulled into the parking lot of the hospital. She entered through the emergency room and made her way to the west wing, which housed the intensive care unit. She might not be able to get into the ICU, but she could badger the hell out of any doctor or nurse coming down the hall, keep at them until she wore them down enough to get some information on Simon.

The second she came through the door of the waiting room and found Courtney, her face red, eyes wet and swollen, Liz knew Simon had taken a turn for the worse.

The sky was still a predawn gray when Courtney slipped behind the garage to smoke a joint. She was so messed up she thought she might fly right out of her skin.

Dr. Greenberg had insisted Courtney and her father go home and get some rest, insisted Simon's condition was stable for now. They planned to go back to the hospital later that morning. Courtney knew she should try to get some sleep, but she was too wired. Even the marijuana wasn't helping.

Last night Simon had almost died. Courtney had been alone in the room with him, holding his hand, hoping his finger would move for her the way it had for Liz Shapiro. Suddenly she saw one of the colored lines on the monitor go from sharp pointed mountains to gentle sloping hills, then almost flat.

Three nurses and two doctors came through the door so fast Courtney thought they had materialized out of thin air. One of the nurses wheeled a crash cart in front of her. Another slapped a blue switch—marked Code 99—on the wall above Simon's bed, while the third took Courtney's arm and tried to escort her to the waiting room. But Courtney held back. She demanded to know what was going on.

"You can't be in here," the nurse said. She put her hands on Courtney's shoulders and attempted to steer her through the door. "Let's let the doctors do their job, okay?"

Courtney hated the woman's condescending tone. She wasn't stupid, for god's sake. She knew there was every chance Simon had just died. And not one of those people would let her be with him. Simon needed someone to call him back. She didn't know why she thought this, but she did. The feeling was so strong that she'd begun to scream Simon's name as loudly as she could. Three or four times she managed to call him, while her flailing arms battled back the startled nurse. Another nurse came to help the first, and between them they all but lifted Courtney off the floor and carried her out of the room.

She sat all night in the cramped waiting room, while her father paced the halls of the hospital and the surrounding grounds, stopping in the cafeteria for an occasional cup of coffee. She made notes in a pocket notebook she took with her to the hospital each day. She had taken to asking the nurses all kinds of questions: about the equipment, the med station, about comas. She'd about worn out her welcome in the intensive care unit. She could tell by the looks on the nurses' faces each time she came through those double metal doors. But she didn't much care. If something happened to Simon, if he died in this place as their mother had, Courtney had notes, a log. She had information. Maybe evidence. They weren't going to get away with this twice.

Courtney took a long toke from her joint and looked out beyond the field. The sycamore in the cemetery was black with crows. A streak of sunlight appeared on the dark horizon, bathing the headstones in orange light. She couldn't help thinking how Simon had almost ended up there, in a plot right next to their mother. He still might. It had taken the doctors two hours to finally stabilize him.

They had gotten this news a few minutes after Liz Shapiro had come storming into the waiting room. Courtney had been so upset about Simon, it never occurred to her how odd it was for Liz to be there at four in the morning. And not once did Liz offer an explanation, tell her why she'd suddenly appeared out of nowhere.

Even worse, she'd totally lost it. She'd let Liz put her

arm around her, had soaked Liz's T-shirt with her tears. But when Liz asked about Simon, about what had happened, Courtney had stiffened and sat upright.

"Why don't you ask him yourself?" she snapped. "You're the one he seems to be communicating with. Maybe he can spell it all out for you with his finger. You know, draw letters in your hand or something." The hurt on Liz's face had only made it worse. Courtney had to look away. She had no idea why she was being such a jerk.

She took another toke of her joint and stared out over the cemetery. The crows lifted out of the sycamore, hundreds of them, and flew toward her. When they reached her backyard, they formed a swirling circle overhead, like an upside-down funnel cloud. If Courtney didn't know better, she might have thought she was looking down into a whirlpool instead of up at the sky. She had the eerie feeling of being sucked up into the air. That was the exact moment she squashed the joint into the dirt and headed for the back door.

Chapter 13

IT WAS ALMOST DAWN. A HEAVY MIST HOVERED ABOVE the ground. A few yards away, four men surrounded Jessup Wildemere beneath the Liberty Tree. One of the men pulled Jessup's hands behind him and tied his wrists with leather thongs. Simon stood nearby, unable to move or speak.

He was just beginning to understand that there had been no trial. Jessup had not been kept in the jail overnight. He had not been tried in the local tavern. Simon knew this because the blood soaking Jessup's clothes was still wet. The men had found him waiting here for Hannah and were going to execute him with their own hands. And Simon was sure the reason they had come here in such short order was because Hannah Dobbler had told them exactly where to find Jessup.

He forced his body to take a step forward, out of the mist. Jessup looked over at him, his expression distant. Simon realized that the other men, who all wore clothes similar to Jessup's, had no idea he was there.

One of the men asked Jessup if he wanted to pray. Jessup stared straight at him, saying nothing. Another man bound Jessup's ankles with thongs. Jessup turned his gaze back to Simon. When their eyes met, Simon felt the surface of his skin buzz and the fine hair on his arms stand straight up as if he were surrounded by an electrical current. He wanted to look away, but Jessup held him with his eyes.

Simon could not stop what had already taken place more than two hundred years earlier. His stomach lurched as one of the men put the rope around Jessup's neck and tossed it over a low branch; another tied the end to his saddle. There would be no drop, only the backward step of the horse pulling Jessup a few inches from the ground.

It was a messy affair. The sight of Jessup's jerking, twisting body, his face swelling, black with congestion, eyes bulging, brought Simon to his knees. He could barely breathe, himself. He squeezed his eyes shut.

The spasmodic strangling sounds stopped, and when Simon looked up, the four men had vanished. Only he and Jessup remained in the gray dawn.

The wind began to blow so fiercely Jessup Wildemere's body swayed back and forth like a pendulum.

Simon sat on the ground and leaned back against the oak, eye level with Jessup's boots, for what seemed like an eternity. The gray dawn finally gave way to the glare of midmorning, a sharp intense light that made his eyes ache.

He wanted to let himself off the hook. He knew there was nothing he could have done to stop the hanging. Still, his stomach continued to churn so badly he was sure he was going to be sick. But it was the tears that truly caught him off guard. They dripped off his chin and left splotches on his hospital gown. He cried for Jessup, for what couldn't be undone, and most of all, for the injustice. An innocent man had died. His only crime had been to fall in love with the wrong woman.

Simon, his back against the tar-coated wound, thought of all the things Jessup could have done differently, not the least of which would have been to leave town before the men came to arrest him. But all he'd cared about was Hannah.

He stared up at the body that had once housed Jessup Wildemere, at the open mouth, the swollen tongue, the bulging eyes, the engorged plum-colored face. He knew Jessup believed himself to be a partner in the murder of Cornelius Dobbler, although he'd had no way of knowing Hannah would kill her own father. Nor had he ever held the knife in his own hands. Still, if they had not fallen in love, none of this would have happened. From the look on Jessup's face, right before the men hanged him, Simon could tell Jessup had accepted his fate, maybe even believed himself guilty. But he also knew, when Jessup had held him with his gaze in those last few seconds, that he wanted something from Simon. The men who took Jessup's life had broken the law. There had been no trial, no jury, no judge. Jessup had been hanged without benefit of counsel and without mercy. What Jessup wanted, what anyone in his position would want, as Simon saw it, was justice.

But how was he going to right a two-hundred-year-old wrong? The men who had hanged Jessup were nothing but moldering dust.

A deep anger welled up in Simon. He was furious at Jessup for being so stupid. "This was your *life*," he shouted to the empty shell overhead. He raised his fist in the air, punched at it in a rage. "You blew it, man. You really *blew* it!"

He leaned sideways, turning away from the sight hanging a few feet away, and pressed one palm against the gash in the tree. He felt the jagged edge of the scar as he got to his feet. Suddenly the memory of that night—the night of the accident—came crashing into his mind. Simon thought his heart might stop beating. For in that moment he knew his foot hadn't come down on the gas pedal by mistake. He knew he could have slammed on the brakes as soon as he realized what was happening, could have lessened the impact. But in that split second, with the tree looming ahead of him, he had seen his chance, his way out, and gone for it.

Liz was in the hospital cafeteria. She was on her third cup of coffee since she'd arrived early that morning. A plate of cold, half-eaten scrambled eggs and toast sat in front of her.

Courtney and her father had gone home to get a few hours of sleep and would be back later. But Liz couldn't bring herself to leave. All her instincts told her Simon wasn't out of the woods yet. The doctors might have stabilized him, but that didn't mean he couldn't slip away from them again.

She wished she had brought something with her to read; even Lucinda Alderman's daily account of her boring, backbreaking life would have been better than nothing. Liz was sorry she didn't have her notebook with her. She could have been working on her oral report, which was scheduled for Tuesday.

She would have to give one fantastic, knock-their-socks-off presentation on Jessup Wildemere if she was going to save her grade in history. The paper she'd dashed off in the wee hours of Friday morning might net her a C if Mrs. Rosen was in a generous mood. But more than likely Liz thought she would end up with a C minus. She didn't doubt for a minute she deserved it. It was her own fault for not reading Lucinda's diary as soon as she'd brought it home. The journal had ended up having far more information than she could have ever processed in those few hours before she had to turn in her paper.

Liz felt in her pocket for a pen. Nothing. She wondered if there was one in the glove compartment out in the car, then decided to see if the woman behind the counter had one. The woman, whose eyes were ringed with dark liner, rummaged around beneath the counter and found an extra pencil. Liz grabbed a handful of paper napkins from the dispenser and returned to her table. She planned to use this waiting time to make notes on how she wanted to present her findings to the class on Tuesday.

She hoped Mrs. Rosen would be as blown away as she had been when she discovered how Lucinda Alderman had suspected Jessup was falling in love with Hannah Dobbler. Hannah Dobbler, Cornelius's daughter, had been engaged to their neighbor, Elias Belcher. Lucinda had worried about what Hannah's father or Elias Belcher would do if they found out. But Lucinda had been afraid to say anything to Jessup. She didn't want him to know she suspected anything.

Liz had actually leaped off her bed and danced around the room when she finally came upon a passage about Jessup's hanging.

> *Joseph has gone back to cut down Jessup's body. He will bury Jessup beneath the tree where he was hanged, although it is not hallowed ground. Reverend Townsend will not allow a murderer to be buried in the churchyard.*
>
> *I cannot understand why Thomas Byrnes and the others could not wait for a judge to be summoned from Trenton. It would have been a matter of only a few months at most. Instead, they took it upon themselves to do what they called "God's will." They would not listen to*

Joseph, who tried to reason with them. They hanged poor Jessup within minutes of tracking him down.

Joseph has told me the men found Jessup sitting beneath the oak near the boundary of our land. He thinks Jessup may have been waiting for Hannah. The poor lad made no attempt to run away. Such news troubles me. I have not been able to sleep for thinking of it. This has been a dark day, indeed, for the people of Havenhill.

Liz had sat on her bed, the journal open on her lap. She shook her head in wonder. Somewhere nestled within the roots of the Hanging Tree, perhaps beneath the asphalt or under the sidewalk, rested the remains of Jessup Wildemere, undisturbed for more than two hundred years. Like everyone else in Bellehaven, she might well have walked over his bones hundreds of times, maybe thousands, considering she passed by the tree every day on her way to school. As if this wasn't unsettling enough, the journal entry that followed, written two days later, was even more disturbing.

I stood by Hannah Dobbler at her father's funeral yesterday morning. She looked as white as the corpse, with eyes as dark and vacant. She never spoke a word, though everyone in attendance stopped to pay their respects.

Sarah Byrnes, whose husband had been

present at the execution, told me that it was Hannah herself who came pounding on their door in the middle of the night. Sarah said the poor girl was covered in blood and weeping hysterically. She gave Sarah and Thomas a horrifying account of how she had tried to stop Jessup from killing her father but had run from the house, fearing for her own life and the lives of her brothers. Such a painful tragedy for one so young. I pray for her daily. May the Lord grant her strength to see her through these dark days.

We brought food to the Dobbler house after the burial, and sat with Hannah and her siblings. Still, she did not speak. It was as if no one else was in the room. To have lost her father and Jessup (if he and Hannah were indeed in love) in one night is a tragedy beyond words.

Two days have passed since the hanging and still I cannot sleep. Jessup comes to me in dreams. His mouth moves, but like Hannah's, no words come out.

Though I have not said so to anyone, out of respect for the Dobbler family, I do not believe Jessup murdered Cornelius. Despite Hannah Dobbler's account and the blood they found on Jessup, I know in my heart it was not in his sweet nature to commit such a foul and horrible deed.

Liz paced her bedroom as she read this last entry. When she had finished it, she sat on the edge of the bed and held the open journal in her lap, tried to take it all in. She reread it several times. To all appearances, Jessup did indeed kill Cornelius Dobbler. But why? Was it because Hannah's father had promised her to Elias Belcher? Killing the father of one's beloved wouldn't exactly endear him to her. Maybe Jessup had been provoked by Cornelius. Or maybe Cornelius had attacked him. Maybe it was self-defense.

And so it had gone. Liz had more questions after her discovery than she had before she found the journal. In the end, with only a few hours before school, she had pounded away at the keyboard and printed out an eight-page paper, half of which was comprised of direct quotes from Lucinda Alderman's diary. The paper was supposed to be at least fifteen pages.

Liz pushed the cold scrambled eggs around the plate with her fork, lost in thought. Forget the C minus. She'd be lucky if Rosen gave her a D plus.

When Devin came to the hospital later that morning with her father, she was surprised to find Liz Shapiro in the waiting room outside the intensive care unit, slouched in one of the chairs, her head against the wall, sleeping. Liz looked as if she'd spent the night in the chair. Her clothes were wrinkled and her hair was an uncombed tangle. Devin suspected Liz was there because of Simon and wondered if there had been a change in his condition. She thought of waking her to ask but decided against it.

She took a seat directly across from Liz, while her father headed to the ICU to see his mother. Later it would be Devin's turn. She knew they would be there the entire day, and that was fine with her. Now that she had legitimate access to the ICU, she hoped to slip in to see Simon, even if it was for just a few minutes. He was as much on her mind these days as her grandmother.

A short time later Courtney walked in. The moment she came through the door, Devin felt an electric charge so powerful it made the hairs on her arms stand straight up and her scalp tingle. Had Courtney felt it too? Had Liz? Devin thought she had seen Liz's legs twitch, although she didn't wake up.

Courtney mumbled "Hi" to Devin and took a seat against the third wall of the small room, while her father went in to see Simon. She and Devin had shared this waiting room quite a bit over the past few days, ever since Devin's grandmother had been moved to the ICU. But they had little to say to each other.

Devin looked from Courtney to Liz and realized that the three of them were each seated in front of a different wall. The room was scarcely eight feet wide. If the girls stretched out their legs, their feet would have met in the middle. This seating arrangement struck her as odd, almost territorial. But then, it wasn't as if they were friends.

"How's Simon?" she asked Courtney.

Courtney looked over at her as if she was considering how to answer this question. "He almost died last night."

"Oh my god." Devin leaned forward. "What happened? Is he okay now?"

Liz woke to the sound of voices. Her muscles ached from sleeping in the chair. She pulled herself up and stretched her stiff legs in front of her.

Courtney was in the middle of giving Devin an account of how the mountains on the monitor had suddenly gone flat, how Simon had died right in front of her, and how the doctors had managed to bring him back. Liz had already heard the story. But she could see that Devin was badly shaken by the news.

When Courtney finished her story and had answered all Devin's questions—the ones she could answer—the three girls leaned back in their seats and resumed their silence. Throughout the day, they went their separate ways. They got coffee in the cafeteria and browsed in the gift shop, looking for nothing in particular except to kill time until it was again their turn to visit, except for Liz, who wasn't allowed into the ICU.

By midafternoon Simon's condition hadn't changed. It was still critical. Liz stared down at her sneakers. She wondered if she should go home. Devin and Courtney had legitimate reasons to be there. But didn't she belong there too? She was Simon's best friend. She loved him. Surely that was reason enough. And there was another reason. She had come because of the disturbing dream she'd had earlier that day. She had come because she was afraid for Simon.

In the end, she decided to stay. It didn't matter what the others thought. Whatever happened, she would be there, waiting.

Liz closed her eyes and tried to sleep again. The image

of Simon swimming in the muddy river came back to her in a rush. She saw him struggling, fighting to keep from being swept away. Up ahead was the oak tree, only a few feet from his grasp. *The branches, Simon,* she whispered. *Grab the branches.*

The sun hovered just above the trees. Soon the sky would darken and Simon would be alone in this place. He had never been there for an entire day. And he was beginning to think he might never leave. Perhaps he would remain there for all eternity with Jessup's silent corpse. He couldn't remember when he had felt so desperate.

Above him three crows circled the tree. Simon watched as they landed on the top branches. For reasons he couldn't begin to explain, he felt he should try to climb this tree. It was stupid, he knew. When he got to the top, then what? He'd just have to come back down again. And there would be Jessup, waiting for him.

One of the crows swooped down to the lowest branch, where Jessup's body hung. There was no mistaking that its urgent caws were for Simon. He laughed at the bird. "Do you think I'm nuts?" he said, as if they were having an actual conversation. "That tree's got to be a hundred feet tall."

One of the other crows landed right on his head and gave his hair a gentle tug. The third remained on the top branch, watching him. Simon sighed and shoved the bird off his head. It settled next to the other crow on the first branch. The branch was almost seven feet from the ground. Simon looked up at the crows and shook his head. "Fine, great, you win," he said.

He wrapped his arms around the base as far as they would go, dug his toes into the rough bark, and began to shinny slowly up the tree. The way Simon was beginning to see it was, there were two ways out of this place: you either pulled yourself up or you let them hang you.

The first few feet of the oak base were the most difficult. The bark tore at his flesh, scraped his hands and feet. But he continued to climb, digging his toes into the crevices of the bark. Some pieces flaked away, causing his foot to slip, but he hung on until finally he reached the first branch, the one Jessup Wildemere's corpse dangled from. One of the crows settled on the branch next to him and cocked its head first to one side, then to the other, as if waiting for something.

Simon took a breath and looked down at Jessup one last time. Kyle and Danny would think Jessup was a real loser. But Simon knew that the man's death, for all the false historic records and local tales, was an honorable one. If he ever got home, he would do everything he could to set the record straight.

From here on, Simon moved carefully from one branch to the next. Two of the crows kept one branch ahead of him; the third waited at the top. With each movement, each grasp of the next branch, another painful memory coursed through him. He remembered Kyle telling him how he'd overheard Principal Schroder talking to George McCabe about a computer security problem. He remembered thinking it would be only a matter of time before McCabe discovered the keystroke recorder program, remembered how he and Kyle had worked like crazy to uninstall the software from three of the school's computers. He remembered feeling sick about what he had done, and how easy it had been for the others to flatter him into showing off what he was capable of. Although he had been mostly showing off for Devin. Devin. These were the most painful memories of all. Because they were also his happiest and he knew such moments would never come again.

He had no illusions about what would be waiting for him when he got back. Possibly criminal charges, his father's fury, the town's stunned shock, and who knew what else. He knew he hadn't actually hacked into the school's network. Hacking was definitely a criminal offense. But he wasn't sure how the school administrators would handle a situation like this. He had, after all, used software to obtain several teachers' passwords, then accessed their computers and printed out exams for his friends. When he had finally gotten his hands on George McCabe's password, it was carte blanche. He could log on to any place in the system, any account. He figured he would probably be expelled for something like that. Still, no matter how bad it got, he'd find a way to live with it. It was better than the alternative. It was better than being dead.

Simon reached out and pulled himself to the next branch. The physical pain was becoming unbearable. With each movement, red-hot wires coursed through his body in place of his veins. He would have screamed if he could. But his jaw was locked tight.

Fragments of memories, of Kyle, Danny, and Devin, of the past year, of all he had done, images of the frogs, the night of the accident, every horrifying moment, seared through his brain.

Some part of him knew he could stop the agony. And then there would be only the fog, the gray nothing. But he had already come this far.

Each branch was more of a struggle than the one before it. He was exhausted. He didn't think he could climb much farther. He stopped to catch his breath, pressed his forehead against the tree. He felt dizzy. The pain was so fierce, Simon thought he might faint and fall, landing on the asphalt or sidewalk.

When he looked up again, the sky was swirling with crows. The birds circled so fast, Simon felt as if he were staring into an upside-down tornado. The faster the birds spun, the more Simon felt himself being pulled upward.

Near the top, the branches were thinner and precariously flexible. Simon stayed close to the base. He wedged his feet into the crooks. The three crows now sat on the uppermost branches. They cawed loudly and flew into the air to join the others as Simon pulled himself to the very top. Overhead hundreds of goldfinches circled between the crows, coming to land on the branches. Their fluttering yellow wings flickered as they descended. Simon, too, flung his arms outward, and all of them, together, caught the golden rays of the setting sun in one glorious burst of light.

Simon didn't realize, until he felt someone's hands on his shoulders, gently pressing him down, that he was screaming, shrieking as loudly as any newborn pulled from the womb. And he did not stop until he felt a sharp prick in his arm and cool waves wash over him as he squinted, dizzy with the morphine, into the bright light above his hospital bed.

Chapter 14

THE NIGHT SIMON GRAY RETURNED FROM THE DEAD, the crows dispersed into the air like a black mist dissolving. Only the occasional black feathers, found floating in glasses of iced tea or clinging to the sticky leaves of petunias, reminded the people of Bellehaven of those two strange weeks in April.

There were no more cases of the West Nile virus, and soon the news crews and the people from the National Institutes of Health drifted out of town as silently as they had arrived, in search of more interesting events. Only the local businesses, which had fared well during the past week, were sorry to see them go.

People no longer talked of curses or black magic. Frogs, crows, heat waves, snowstorms, viruses—they were the stuff of everyday life. Now they shook their heads in wonder and joked about how Nature had gone haywire. They laughed over how so many of the residents had panicked and left town, although it was a nervous kind of laughter, the kind made by elementary-school boys daring each other to walk through the cemetery after midnight.

By Monday morning everyone at Bellehaven High knew Simon Gray had come out of his coma, and they were relieved. But the real talk was about George McCabe. Word had spread that he had confessed to giving his password to some of the seniors on the football team, allowing them to log on to the Net and download porn. It was only one of many passwords he used, but its most treasured feature was that he had set up the account to bypass the firewall designed to screen out undesirable sites.

The whole school was in an uproar. Rumors began to circulate that the police had been investigating a breach in the computer security system and that Simon Gray had been under suspicion, although no one believed for a minute that Simon could ever be involved in something like that.

Now the finger seemed to be pointing at half the football team, a few of whom had athletic scholarships for the fall. Any one of them, or all of them, for that matter, could have used Mr. McCabe's password to get into the system. They would be able to print out exams, change grades, do whatever they wanted, although each of them had vehemently denied this.

The situation became far worse than anyone could have imagined when Roger Garvey pointed out to Principal

Schroder that the boys under suspicion could have shared this password with any number of other people, who in turn could have used the knowledge to secure all sorts of information—not the least of which might be exams—from the school's system. It was as if a computer virus had spread through the entire school, contaminating each and every student. There was nothing left to do but change everyone's password and hope for the best.

That was when the board of ed got involved and the superintendent recommended proceeding with caution. This was, according to him, "a rather delicate matter." The parents of the implicated members of the football team were nearly apoplectic—especially those whose sons had athletic scholarships. They were, in fact, more upset over their sons' losing their financial aid than they were about their boys' being accused of downloading pornography on the school computers.

By now everyone was saying George McCabe had probably given the police Simon's name just to get the monkey off his back. And while they were glad Simon was no longer under suspicion, no one was happy about a week's suspension for half the football team, either.

Nobody, however, was the least bit surprised to learn that George McCabe had turned in his resignation first thing that morning before classes began. It seemed that two of the senior football team members were still under age eighteen. Exposing minors to pornography, as George McCabe had learned, was a criminal offense.

Liz Shapiro couldn't wait to tell Simon what was going on. He would probably get a good laugh out of it, especially the rumors about his being under investigation. How could anyone even think Simon might have been involved in all this nasty computer business? She knew him better than that.

Liz was so relieved to have him back, she skipped eighth period and headed straight to the hospital.

Like everyone else at school, Devin McCafferty was stunned by the news about Alan Caldwell and some of the other senior football players. But she had no illusions about her own situation. Their actions, however wrong, were separate from the ones she'd been involved in. Still, it would have been pointless for her to go to the authorities and confess her own misdeeds. It wouldn't have any impact on the outcome of this latest case. All she would accomplish would be to get Simon and the others in deep trouble. And she couldn't bring herself to do that. Although she was sorely tempted when Kyle cornered her outside art class and made a joke about what happened to people who tried to play the game and got careless.

Before Devin broke up with him, they would have been heading down to the cafeteria for lunch. Now she looked him straight in the eye, as if he were a total stranger. "I hate what we've been doing," she said. "I hate this whole business."

Kyle glanced nervously up and down the hall to make sure no one had heard her. He took her by the arm and gently ushered her back into the art room. No one was there. He closed the door.

Devin stood with her back against a metal supply cabinet and let her backpack drop to the floor. Kyle leaned toward her. He put the palms of his hands on the cold metal just above her shoulders, as if he were going to kiss her. But the expression on his face suggested that kissing was the last thing on his mind.

"Look, Dev, I know things haven't been good between us lately. But this isn't just about me. If you're thinking about unburdening your conscience, consider what it would do to Simon and Danny."

It was all she could do not to laugh in his face. "You're right, I'd never do that to Simon. So you can relax."

Kyle pushed himself away from the cabinet and cocked his head at her. "Is that the reason you broke it off with me? Simon?"

Devin rolled her eyes toward the ceiling. "No. I broke it off with you because of *you*." She recovered her backpack and started for the door.

"I don't see what the big deal is. We didn't get caught. We won't, either, as long as Simon keeps his mouth shut. No one got hurt. And you're going to Cornell next fall."

Her hand was already on the doorknob. She glanced back at him. "I'm not going to Cornell."

"Middlebury, then. Whatever."

"Or Middlebury. If they'll take me, I'm going to the community college."

Kyle stared at her, dumbfounded.

Devin was amused by the look on his face. It took a lot to get a rise out of Kyle. She knew this from experience.

"Why would you do that? You worked hard to get into those schools."

"But I *didn't* work hard. That's the point." She yanked open the door and stepped into the hall. Kyle was right behind her.

"Your SAT scores were yours. You worked hard for those. And what about all those extracurricular activities? Jeez, Dev."

"I need time to figure out what I want to do. Okay?"

He shook his head. "But community college instead of Cornell? You're throwing away the chance of a lifetime. What the hell are you thinking?"

Devin sighed and looked away. " 'To know my deed, 'twere best not know myself.' "

"What?"

"Nothing. It's a line from *Macbeth*."

The bell ending lunch period echoed through the halls.

"I've got French," Devin said as kids came storming out of the classrooms, flooding the hall.

After school, Devin stopped at the community college to pick up an application. She felt not even the slightest twinge of regret as she sat on the bus, on her way to the hospital, filling out the forms. She was looking forward to seeing her grandmother, who had come out of her coma only a few hours after Simon had rejoined the living.

Jeff Cole, the physical therapist, lifted Simon's leg, gently bent it at the knee, laid it back down, then lifted the other.

He was a barrel-chested man with a booming, overly enthusiastic voice, who tended to bounce on his sneakers when he walked. He told Simon he was making terrific progress. Simon let him talk. He knew there would be more weeks of physical therapy ahead.

Every day people came to see him, Liz and Devin, even Danny on two occasions. And of course, his father and Courtney. Courtney came after school and stayed until their father showed up. Then she left.

Over and over he listened to everyone's take on what had happened in Bellehaven over the past few weeks. Simon recalled the night of the accident, how hordes of peepers had exploded out of nowhere. None of this surprised him. Not the blizzard, the heat waves, the mosquitoes, or the West Nile virus. And especially not the crows.

Kyle was the only one who didn't come by. Simon hadn't expected him to. He wasn't of any use to Kyle anymore—although Kyle had called him twice to make sure he wasn't going to tell anyone about "the project" now that he had returned from the dead.

It was Courtney who told Simon how he had caused a sensation, coming out of his coma the way he had. According to the nurse, who had been changing his IV bag, Simon bolted straight up in bed, eyes wide open, and began to scream like a banshee. Apparently it was extremely unusual for patients to wake up from a coma that way, unless the coma had been intentionally drug induced by the doctors, using pentobarbital to prevent swelling in the brain. That hadn't been the case with Simon. The story was all over the hospital. Even the ladies at the information desk knew about it.

Courtney also told him how the police had confiscated his PC. "Dad told me he'd ground me for life if I said anything to anyone about the cops coming to our house and that you were under suspicion. Like anybody'd ever believe that anyway," Courtney said. "Simon the Good in trouble with the law?" She shook her head and laughed. "I don't think so."

Simon never so much as blinked as he listened to his sister go on about the afternoon Lieutenant Santino and Sergeant Fowler showed up at the front door. He knew there was nothing in his computer related to "the project." Nothing that would convict him, although it made him uncomfortable to know that some total stranger might have read his poems or stories.

Danny related his own version of what he'd dubbed the McCabe Porn Caper. Simon didn't share his relief.

It was true that George McCabe had brought the whole mess on himself. Still, Simon didn't kid himself about his own role in Mr. McCabe's tragedy. None of this would have happened if he hadn't set in motion a series of events that resulted in a police investigation of the school's computer network.

Simon would have liked nothing better than to go to the police and tell them what he had done. But because Kyle had decided to follow through, to attend Harvard in the fall, Simon would carry his secret to the grave. He'd given his word to Kyle. Enough lives had been ruined lately. And there were Danny and Devin to consider.

Danny had gone from a solid A in physics to a C in just two weeks and had more or less tossed in the towel. He knew his acceptance by Dartmouth was going down the tubes right along with his grades that marking period. In his own way, he seemed relieved. He told Simon he planned to go to California that summer, maybe apply to some schools out there.

Devin, too, had chosen a different route.

The day before, when the McCaffertys had come to take Devin's grandmother home, Devin stopped in to see him. She sat at the foot of his bed, looking more beautiful than Simon could ever remember, her red hair shimmering in the sunlight from the window, and told him she was going to the community college in the fall. She was smiling, looking more relaxed and happy than he had seen her in a long time. She didn't have to explain her decision. Simon understood exactly why she'd done it. Secretly, he was glad she wouldn't be going away to school next year, especially since she'd told him she'd broken up with Kyle.

Any chance he had with Devin was a long shot. But hadn't he just beaten the odds? Hadn't he returned from the dead? Maybe he had good reason to hope.

He wondered if Devin would visit him as often as she had over the past few days, now that her grandmother was no longer in the hospital. He doubted it. But then, the very next afternoon, after school, there she was, standing in his doorway, holding one of the school's laptops. She had talked Dr. Schroder into letting Simon use it while he was recovering. Simon chose to take Devin's unexpected visit as a good sign.

In a few days the tutor his father had hired would begin coming each morning. Simon would have assignments to complete, work to keep him busy. He looked forward to it. He had too much time on his hands right now. Too much time to think about the past.

And there was something else, something that hovered on the edge of his consciousness, a dream he'd had while in the coma. The image of Jessup Wildemere continued to haunt him. It was so vivid and alive that at times Simon found it difficult to convince himself the time he'd spent with Jessup wasn't real.

The next day, when Liz showed up after school, she said, "You know that stupid paper I had to do for Mrs. Rosen?" She parked herself at the foot of Simon's bed.

"The one on Jessup Wildemere?" Simon wondered if maybe the whole Jessup experience had been nothing more than an illusion triggered by Liz. She'd spent half the marking period talking to him about her paper. It seemed like a reasonable enough explanation. So why was his heart pounding so loudly the sound almost blocked his ears?

Liz nodded and pulled a book from her backpack. The cover was leather, worn and cracked in places. "Well, I blew it big-time. She gave me a D plus. She said it read as if I'd written it in my sleep. Which isn't all that far from the truth. But I redeemed myself with my oral report. A plus. You would have enjoyed it. I had them spellbound. Nobody could believe what I'd found out."

Simon didn't say a word; he just listened as Liz told him how she'd all but given up on her paper, when a week before it was due, she'd found a journal.

Lucinda Alderman's journal. Joseph Alderman's wife. The man whose fence Jessup had helped to build. Simon was stunned. Joseph Alderman had actually existed.

"I can't believe I lucked out like this," Liz said. She turned the pages of the journal to a place she had marked with a slip of paper. "You know how everybody thinks Jessup killed Cornelius Dobbler and after he was tried in the tavern, the residents of this fine town took him out and hanged him?"

Simon barely nodded.

"Well, all those tales are just that: tales. Actually, tall tales is more like it." Liz bent over the book and began to read the passage about Jessup's coming to work for Joseph. She read Lucinda's account of Jessup's appearance—a comely and well-educated young man—and how she suspected that Jessup was falling in love with Hannah Dobbler. She read how Joseph had buried him beneath the Liberty Tree on the outskirts of their land, and about the funeral for Cornelius Dobbler.

The real account was even worse than Simon could have imagined. Hannah hadn't just told the men where to find Jessup, she had accused him of murdering her father. If Liz hadn't been there, Simon might have let himself cry. No one else, except perhaps Lucinda Alderman, as far as he knew, had shed tears for Jessup Wildemere.

When Liz had read all the marked passages, she closed the journal. "Incredible, huh? They hanged him without a trial, like some wild-ass bunch of vigilantes."

"They murdered an innocent man," Simon told her.

"Well, not exactly," Liz said, shifting her weight and

slipping the journal into her backpack. "That's only Lucinda's take on it."

Simon wanted to tell Liz that Lucinda's take was probably as close to the truth as anyone had gotten. He wanted to tell her about Jessup, about the time he had spent with him while he was in the coma. But in the end, all he said was "You need to let people know what really happened."

"I did, in my oral report. And it's all in the paper I handed in to Rosen."

"No. I mean, write a story for the local paper or something. You have the evidence." He pointed toward her backpack.

Liz shrugged. "I guess I could make copies of the pages before I sneak the journal back where I found it."

"Show them."

"Who?"

"The people at the historical society. Show them what you found."

"Oh, right, like anybody in this town is going to want to hear how the only hanging that ever took place in the entire county might have been a murder. That's not the kind of dirty laundry people like to see airing on their clotheslines."

Simon knew all about keeping secrets, about hiding the truth. He had his own dirty laundry stashed away in a mental hamper.

Liz stared down at her backpack. She let out a deep sigh. "Well . . . there was this reporter from *The Star-Ledger* here last week, covering the West Nile virus story. He mentioned the Wildemere legend in his article. He might be interested. I could send him the information I have."

"Do it, okay? Tell him what you discovered."

"Why? What's the big deal?"

"Just do it to make things right."

That night, Simon began to write a poem about Jessup Wildemere. When he thought about the night of the accident, the image of a shadowy figure standing in front of the Liberty Tree crept into his memory. He remembered how the form had taken the shape of a man in his headlights. Even before Simon's foot had hit the gas, the dark shape had been there. Maybe the shadowy form had been Jessup's spirit. Or maybe it was nothing more than a shadow created by the glare of the headlights. Only in this poem would Simon allow himself to give voice to what he could not quite bring himself to believe, that Jessup's soul had been waiting there, beneath the oak tree, all along, waiting more than two hundred years to tell someone his story, waiting for someone to set the record straight.

Then, one day at the end of May, just when the people of Bellehaven had begun to breathe a little easier, a story about Jessup Wildemere appeared in *The Star-Ledger.* The story had been written by a staff reporter and quoted pages from Lucinda Alderman's journal.

The residents of Bellehaven flew into an uproar all over again, insisting that Lucinda Alderman's account was subjective and therefore flawed. They showed the brief account in the court records to prove their point. They claimed Jessup Wildemere was a murderer who was brought to justice. After all, they said, people did things differently in those days.

No one knew whom to believe.

As if that weren't bad enough, a mysterious bronze plaque had appeared next to the Liberty Tree, a few feet from the original plaque. The inscription sent the town into a frenzy of denial.

> **In 1798 Jessup Wildemere,**
> **an innocent man falsely accused,**
> **was hanged from this tree**
> **without benefit of trial or counsel**
> **by the good people of Havenhill.**

No one knew who had put it there. But the people of Bellehaven were bound and determined it wouldn't stay. Special meetings of the town council were held. Petitions were signed. Letters to the editor flooded the offices of the *Bellehaven Press.* The outrage continued for months. But for some reason, no one ever touched the sign. Perhaps they feared retribution from the ghost of Jessup Wildemere. Perhaps they thought some distant relative had placed the plaque there, and they did not want to cause bad feelings by removing it. Or maybe, just maybe, in their hearts, they suspected there might be a grain of truth to the inscription after all.

Acknowledgments

I am indebted to a number of people who gave generously of their time and experience to help me with the medical and technical details of this book. Any errors, however, are my own. My thanks to Catherine Belfiore; Mary Piso, RN; Barbara Reed, RN; and Lura Burrell, RN, whose son, at age seventeen, spent four days in a coma. Thank you, Lura, for sharing his experience with me. My thanks also to Arlene Olcheski of the New Jersey State Police, and to my teen advisors: Matt Schanbacher, Jaime Schanbacher, and Aaron Weiner.

Special thanks to Laurie Halse Anderson for our daily e-mail exchange during those tense weeks before our deadlines and for being so supportive.

I also wish to thank my agent, Tracey Adams, for reading and commenting on an earlier draft; Pearl Young; and especially my editor, Karen Wojtyla, who skillfully kept me on course without ever taking over the rudder.

My deepest gratitude goes to my personal in-house computer consultant, my husband, Mac, whose support, as always, goes way beyond the technical.

About the Author

Joyce McDonald earned bachelor's and master's degrees in English from the University of Iowa. After working in publishing for fourteen years, she returned to the academic life and earned a Ph.D. in English from Drew University; she taught at both Drew and East Stroudsburg University for several years. She is the author of five other books for children and young adults, including *Shadow People* and *Swallowing Stones,* an ALA Top Ten Best Book for Young Adults. Joyce McDonald lives in northwestern New Jersey with her husband and their cats.